'I've decided ... to do is call of ...

'No, Nick! You c ...
I...gave in to temptation... If neither of us
says anything...and if we make certain to
keep away from each other...'

'I don't know if we can put that sort of
distance between us,' he pointed out finally.
'We have to work together... Anyway, who
says I want this... "whatever-it-is" between us
to die a natural death? Perhaps I want to see if
it can survive and grow.'

She covered her face with her hands. 'But this
isn't about you and me. You can't let a couple
of one-night stands knock your life off
course.'

'Can you really dismiss them as meaningless
roll in the hay?'

'I have to. It doesn't matter that I've never
known anything like it and probably never
will again. I've got to find some way of
parcelling this episode in my life out of sight
before it causes a disaster. Otherwise, I'd
never be able to live with the guilt.'

Dear Reader

A while ago I was lucky enough to spend a week in Cumbria. While I was revisiting places I first came to know when our children were small, I found I was looking at them in a completely different way.

Suddenly the quaint little market town I'd once known so well was growing and turning into the background for a whole new cast of characters working in and around Denison Memorial Hospital. This book is the second in a series of stories about those characters and I hope you enjoy reading about them as much as I enjoy creating them.

Perhaps along the way I can give you a taste of what it was like to live surrounded by such magnificent scenery and the inimitable Cumbrian people. I will certainly be going back again.

Happy reading.

Josie

GUILTY SECRET

BY
JOSIE METCALFE

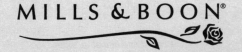

MILLS & BOON®

First published in Great Britain 2001
Harlequin Mills & Boon Limited,
Eton House, 18-24 Paradise Road, Richmond, Surrey TW9 1SR

© Josie Metcalfe 2001

ISBN 0 263 82715 1

Set in Times Roman 10½ on 12 pt.
03-0202-47632

Printed and bound in Spain
by Litografía Rosés, S.A., Barcelona

CHAPTER ONE

'HOME, sweet home,' Nick muttered with a strange flutter of disquiet.

He reversed his new pride and joy into a parking space designated STAFF ONLY and switched the engine off as he glanced at his surroundings.

He'd slotted himself into a line of vehicles and suddenly realised that they all belonged to his new colleagues.

New colleagues, new job, new life.

His stomach tightened at the thought of the giant leap sideways he'd just made in his career and, in spite of the winter chill beginning to seep into the vehicle, he felt the prickle of nervous sweat.

Nicholas Johnson, General Practitioner. He drew in a shaky breath, wondering whether he would be able to live up to the enormous responsibilities the job involved.

He wasn't even certain whether he'd made the right choice or whether it had been made for him. Had he leapt at the idea too hastily?

His life and his mind had been in such turmoil that Jack's unexpected visit had assumed the power to start an avalanche of consequences. A year later, they were still rumbling on and he wasn't certain that he'd come up for air yet.

The tick of the four-by-four's cooling engine broke the silence as he stared out at the view, the distant vista of wide valley floor and sere winter hillsides beginning to work their magic on him. Slowly, the knots inside him started to unravel and he relaxed against the head-rest.

'Yes,' he said quietly, firmly, casting his mind briefly back to the bitter tensions that had surrounded him before he'd made his decision. 'I *have* made the right move. It might have taken me thirty-two years to get there, but my life is on track now.'

He reached across for his painfully new medical bag and climbed out of the car, unable to stop himself taking one last look at it sitting there in all its gleaming cranberry-red splendour. 'A far cry from the sports car you wanted, but eminently more practical around here,' he muttered as he finally turned away.

He paused in front of the entrance and looked up at the neatly incised words. DENISON MEMORIAL HOSPITAL.

It had been two months since he'd first seen them, when he'd come up for his interview. Two months since Jack had taken him on a lightning tour around the small Cumbrian town of Edenthwaite and the surrounding countryside that the hospital served. His old friend had mournfully pointed out all the entertaining possibilities there might have been for the two of them to have fun together further afield, if only Nick hadn't turned so staid.

Staid? Perhaps he had, he thought with a shrug.

Such testosterone-laden roistering had been attractive during their training years but life had moved on since then. He'd made choices, the same as Jack had, but in his case, not all of them had been good and some of them had even threatened his very career.

When he'd finally had his eyes opened to his peril-ous position it had been time to make some hard decisions, and the realisation that Jack's baby sister, Vicky, had completed her nursing training had suddenly assumed a fortuitous significance. He could still hardly believe that now he'd moved to Edenthwaite they would be starting to organise their wedding.

He shivered as the icy January wind found its way between the open edges of his thickly insulated jacket and he stepped through the automatic doors into the welcome warmth of the main reception area.

'Can I help you?' offered the smiling young woman at the desk, her pale coffee skin flawless and her long dark hair in an immaculate plait that must surely have reached all the way to her waist. He flicked a glance at the badge that gave her name as Farah.

'I hope so,' he said with an answering smile. 'Could you direct me to the GP unit? I'm looking for Jack Lawrence.'

'Ah. And you are?' Her glance had dropped to something just out of his sight, probably a computer screen, he thought, and silently applauded their security measures.

'Nick Johnson. I'm the new—'

'GP,' she finished for him with a beaming smile. 'Welcome to Denison Memorial, Dr Johnson.'

'Thank you very much.' His heart lifted. If this was a sample of the way he was going to be accepted by the rest of the staff, he had *definitely* made the right choice in moving here.

'I've had a message left here for you,' Farah continued. 'Dr Lawrence had to go out on an emergency call, but he suggested that you might like to drive over to Dr Long's house to introduce yourself and to pick up the spare mobile phone. Dr Faraday's still doing his afternoon of minor surgery and the rest of the doctors

are either out on home visits or off duty. Oh…' She
leafed through several papers and handed them over.
'Dr Lawrence also left you a copy of the roster for the
next couple of days and said if you haven't organised
yourself a bed for the night, you're welcome to turn
up at his place.'

Nick grinned. That was typical of Jack. He was the
sort of person who would leave such things as accom-
modation to the last minute. That wasn't how Nick
liked to live his life. Not any more. Everything was
going to be meticulously planned and smooth-running
from now on.

'That won't be a problem,' he told the beautiful
young woman. 'I've already got a place and dropped
my things off.' He shared a smile with her that told
him that they both knew what Jack was like. 'Is there
a map I could borrow to find my way to Dr Long's?'

'He's drawn one for you.' She pointed to the small
sheaf in his hands and he separated out the page with
a sketch and some accompanying directions. 'Said to
tell you he'll see you here at eight tomorrow morning
if he doesn't see you sooner, and not to worry because
it'll be an orientation day. They won't be throwing you
in at the deep end. Oh, and could you possibly deliver
these?' She handed over a plastic carrier bag filled with
rolls of wallpaper. 'They were delivered here after Dr
Long went off duty.'

As he made his way back out into the icy wind Nick
wondered whether Vicky was on duty somewhere in
the hospital. Was she expecting him to call on her to
announce his arrival? For a moment he contemplated
the idea of going up to her ward, but he was uncomfortably aware of a nagging sense of reluctance.

'Tomorrow will be soon enough,' he muttered, uncomfortably trying to subdue the feeling that he was dragging his feet.

This wasn't like him, he argued silently as he set off again in search of Dr Long. Once he'd settled on a course of action, he always saw it through, even if doing the right thing jeopardised both his heart and his career. He wouldn't even have been in Edenthwaite if he hadn't stuck to his guns when he'd discovered what one of his most trusted colleagues had been doing; would still have been working in a high-pressure city A and E department instead of beginning a new life as a GP in Cumbria.

So why was he feeling so reluctant to see Vicky? It was nearly two months since they'd last seen each other, and that had only been for a few hours while they'd chosen her ring and celebrated with a meal. Surely he should be eager?

But he wasn't, and that was making him feel guilty and he didn't like the feeling.

The fact that he was also lying awake at night wondering if he was making the most monumental mistake of his life was another thing that was grating on his conscience. Vicky would never understand, not after twelve years of waiting, so there was no way he could even mention his doubts to her.

'What on earth…!'

The directions had said that he wouldn't be able to miss the house because it was the only one on this side of the road for at least a mile once he left Edenthwaite. They hadn't warned him what he'd find in the driveway.

The startling sight of a scantily clad woman wielding a hose to wash her car on a bitterly cold January day was enough to drag him out of his dark thoughts with a jerk.

The tracksuit bottoms were decent enough, even though they were obviously soaked through and clinging to every inch they covered. It was the wet T-shirt that was making his eyes stand out on stalks, revealing a body that could easily win a competition. She wasn't a straight-up-and-down stick insect like those that graced the fashion pages but an honest-to-goodness woman with lush curves in all the right places.

Nick swore softly as every hormone in his body leapt to attention in a way that hadn't happened for a very long time, then swore again when he realised that this was the address he was looking for.

'Down, boy!' he muttered repressively as he applied the brakes, realising with a flash of guilt that he'd never had this sort of reaction to Vicky. Just his luck that he should finally realise what had been missing from his life, and discover at the same time that she must be the wife of one of his new colleagues.

He paused a moment to gather up the ungainly bag of wallpaper, hoping that it would be time enough for the more obvious signs of his appreciation to subside, but as he couldn't take his eyes off her, it didn't work.

There was something utterly fascinating about the way she was soaping and hosing the vehicle to within an inch of its existence without a care for the fact that the bitter wind had tightened her nipples for all to see.

'Control, man,' he muttered, and squeezed his eyes shut. 'Self-control.' He drew in a deep breath and held it for the count of ten, but it made not a scrap of difference.

'OK, no self-control, so fall back on self-defence.' He groaned as he slid out of his seat with the ungainly carrier bag and tried fruitlessly to adjust his clothing. Oh, well, if nothing else he could hold the wallpaper in front of himself to disguise the effect she was having on him.

'Get it over with,' he muttered gruffly. 'You just need to drop this off and pick up the stuff Long's left waiting for you. Thirty seconds, max, and then you can go home for a cold shower.'

'Bastard!' Frankie swore between her teeth as she wielded the soapy sponge over the roof of the car. 'Seven years! Seven years I've had to cope by myself and then he does this to me!'

She squeezed the trigger on the hose and released a high-pressure jet of water to wash the soap away, totally uncaring of the fact that she was already completely drenched by the resulting spray. It was just one more in a long list of much-hated jobs she'd been doing since her precious daughters had waved her goodbye for their once-a-month weekends with their father. Well, until recently it had been once a month if he didn't have anything more exciting going on. The only thing she could be proud of was the fact that she hadn't screamed like a fishwife when the weasel had waited until the very last second to dump his time bomb in her lap.

'For seven years he's been late with every support cheque, probably just so he can have the pleasure of hearing me beg,' she muttered viciously. 'And now that they're old enough to be interesting—old enough to be able to hold a conversation or take out for a meal—now that he's married his perfect trophy wife, he's realised that he doesn't have to ruin her perfect figure to satisfy her urge to play mummy. Oh, no! One saggy overweight wife is enough for him so he's just going to go to court to take possession of the family he's already fathered.'

'Excuse me,' said a deep male voice, and she shrieked in shock, whirling to face the unexpected interloper with the hose firing at maximum pressure.

'Oh…my…God,' she breathed in horror, completely forgetting to release her grip on the trigger as the water hit her visitor squarely in the middle of his chest. The spray bounced off in every direction and in less than a second he was completely soaked from head to foot.

'Oh, I'm sorry!' She swung the hose away from him and finally remembered to release the trigger. 'Oh, I'm *so* sorry!'

'That water's *warm*!' he exclaimed in evident surprise, raking one hand through his hair to stop the water running down his face. The strands were as sleek and dark as mink and threw the lean planes and angles of his face into stark prominence.

'Of course it is!' Frankie retorted distractedly, watching him blink the drops off sinfully long lashes. 'I might be mad but I'm not suicidal.'

To her surprise he laughed, the sound rich and melodious and totally unexpected when the poor man had just been drenched by a lunatic. If it had been Martin…

She shook her head, dismissing her double-dealing ex-husband from her thoughts.

'I really am *so* sorry. I just didn't hear you arrive,' she explained with a grimace as she flicked the hose aside and dropped the nozzle onto the edge of the tatty patch of grass that passed for a lawn. 'Usually I can hear the sound of the gate, but over the noise of the water… Look, you really must come inside and get dry.' She turned to lead the way towards the back door into the house. 'The water starts off warm but it doesn't stay that way very long in this wind.'

'Actually, I only came to deliver this.' He indicated the water-spotted plastic bag, hesitating on the doormat as though not wanting to drip all over her floor. 'And to collect—'

'Oh, is that my wallpaper at last?' She grabbed hold of his elbow to pull him into the warmth of the kitchen, and suddenly appreciated just how cold her hands had become when she realised how warm he was. The contrast was almost as potent as an electric shock and she was so startled that she jerked her hand away in a hurry.

She concentrated on heeling off her disreputable old trainers and her feet squelched audibly as she went across to put the kettle on the hob.

'Could you keep an eye on that while I go and get you something to dry off?' she said hurriedly, having to drag her eyes away from him yet again. 'A towel…or something…'

What was it about this man and his broad shoulders? She was almost mesmerised by the shadowy glimpses of dark hair showing through the wet fabric of his shirt, fascinated by the broad wedge stretching from nipple to nipple and tapering towards the waistband of his trousers.

Before her gaze could sink any lower he had casually changed to a two-handed grip on the plastic bag and she blinked.

Had the manoeuvre been deliberate? Had he noticed the direction her eyes were going and positioned it strategically to prevent her examining any more intimate regions?

Her face was flaming by the time she hurried up the

stairs. What was the matter with her? She hadn't taken
this much interest in a man's body in years. It would
have been all right if she'd been ogling one of the idols
displayed on her daughters' poster-strewn bedroom
walls, but to do it to a strange man standing in her
kitchen...

The fact that he was soaking wet made the situation
both worse and better. Worse, because the state of his
clothing was all her fault, but better, because that sod-
den clothing was now displaying all those lean muscles
almost as clearly as if he'd been naked.

'I can certainly see the attraction of wet T-shirt competitions,' she muttered under her breath as she entered
the bathroom in search of one of her larger towels, and
came to a halt with an agonised squeak as she caught
sight of herself in the mirror.

And she'd thought *his* body had been on display...

She covered her face with her hands and groaned in
mortification as heat poured over her again. She didn't
need to peer between her fingers to confirm the fact
that, in honour of the hated task, she was not only
wearing one of her oldest and thinnest T-shirts, but that
she hadn't bothered wearing a bra underneath it in an-
ticipation of getting soaked. Her wet bra straps had
rubbed her raw the last time she'd tried it.

What she hadn't realised in the course of her ca-
thartic car-washing session had been quite how much
detail was visible through the semi-transparent fabric,
right down to the colour of her areolae and the fact that
her nipples were shamelessly erect.

Frankie groaned again, desperately wishing that she
didn't have to face the man, but she could hardly leave
him dripping in her kitchen, especially when he had
been kind enough to deliver her wallpaper. Anyway,

she had more important things to worry about, like the fact that her ratfink of a lawyer ex-husband was going to try to take her children away from her.

She dithered a moment longer before she peeled the clammy garment over her head and stepped out of her tracksuit bottoms, then quickly towelled the worst of the water off her body. She paused again as her hand hovered over the towelling dressing-gown hanging on the back of the bathroom door. Was it a sensible idea to wear so little in the presence of an absolute stranger?

She gave a snort of derision and shrugged her way into it. According to Martin, she could dance in front of the man stark naked and it couldn't entice him, not since childbirth had ruined whatever charms she'd had.

'Here,' she said as she came back into the kitchen and found Nick reading the various missives posted on the giant pink pig that was their family message-board. She found it immeasurably touching that he'd found an old newspaper to catch the rivulets of water still draining out of his clothes. What was more, he was standing on it in his bare feet, his socks and shoes left abandoned on the mat inside the door.

'I've left a clean towel on the side of the bath,' she continued briskly, determined not to look at the way his saturated clothing was clinging to broad shoulders and long lean legs, or the strange intimacy of his naked feet. 'If you'd like to put this on, I could throw your things in the tumble-dryer.'

'What's this?' He took the bundle of fabric from her and shook it out to reveal the black and gold opulence of an embroidered silk dressing-gown in all its glory. 'Wow! Are you sure you want me to wear this? Won't your husband object?'

For a moment all she was aware of was the smooth

tones of his voice, somewhere between the depths of a baritone and the richness of a tenor, then his question registered.

'What he doesn't know, he can't object to,' she said, her voice sharpened by her recent exchange of words with the rat in question, then realised she needed to explain. 'I bought it for him for Christmas over seven years ago, but before I could even wrap it, he told me he'd found the woman of his dreams and wanted a divorce.'

'And in the circumstances, you decided he didn't deserve to get a present from you that year,' he added with a pleasing touch of irony.

'In the circumstances, no,' she agreed, surprised to feel a grin tugging at the corners of her mouth. 'I thought it was far too good to throw away on a rat.'

'In which case, I thank you for the implied compliment and would be delighted to make use of it—the tumble-dryer, too, if you wouldn't mind. Being new to the area, I haven't got my laundry system sorted out yet. I haven't done any unpacking either, so if the worst comes to the worst, I might have to wear these things to work tomorrow.'

Frankie gave him directions to the bathroom then listened to him padding up the stairs while she took out mugs and milk.

To keep her mind off the disturbing fact that there was a handsome stranger stripping his clothes off in her bathroom she found her thoughts returning to that last conversation with Martin.

He'd looked so cool and controlled in his expensive suit while she'd felt positively frazzled at the end of a frantically busy day. There was also the fact that she absolutely hated the weekends that her daughters spent away from her, weekends that had become far more regular of late.

Usually, Martin waited in the car while Laura and Katie raced around the house to pack the last few things they needed for a weekend with their father. This time, he'd startled her by stepping into the house and making his way unerringly towards the lounge with the air of a visiting dignitary.

Of course, he made certain she saw his raised eyebrows when he saw the state of the room. There was never enough time in the morning to tidy round so there were cushions piled up in untidy heaps where the girls had made themselves comfortable to watch television the previous night. There was also her empty coffee-mug on the corner of the table beside a disorderly pile of journals and the next pile of bills waiting for payment.

Frankie had just realised that the pair of shoes she'd been hunting for that morning had been kicked under the edge of her favourite chair when he'd dropped his bombshell.

She was still staring at the smiling photo of her two precious daughters pinned on the pink pig where she could see them every day when an unmistakably male voice interrupted her nightmare.

'Shall I dump these in the dryer?'

She blinked and glanced down as a lean hand took the jar of coffee out of her white-knuckled grasp and deposited it on the work surface then took the furiously hissing kettle off the hob.

'Are you all right?' he asked, gentle concern clear in his expression.

'Fine,' she choked with a gesture towards the dryer.

'Put the dark things in separately in case the colour runs.'

Nick hesitated a moment before complying silently, his eyes far too intent, far too analytical.

She whirled away to reach for the coffee-jar again and completely missed it, knocking it to the floor with a crash.

'Damn!' She looked down at her bare feet, covered with shards of glass and coffee granules. 'Oh, damn, damn, damn, can this weekend get any worse?' she wailed, her voice rising uncontrollably towards a shriek before she burst into tears.

'Hey! Hey!' he crooned gently as he lifted her up as if she were no bigger than nine-year-old Katie and deposited her on the work surface. 'It's only a jar of coffee. Have you cut yourself?'

Frankie was sobbing helplessly as she watched him through her tears. Somehow it only made things worse that a complete stranger should be bending over her feet to brush them off and check that the glass hadn't cut her.

When was the last time anyone had cared about her, about her welfare, about her happiness? She spent all her days and all her energy caring about her children and her patients so that there was nothing left for herself. And here he was, young, handsome, solvent—if his gorgeous car was any indication—and showing her more consideration than anyone had in years.

And all she could do was humiliate herself by sobbing her heart out.

'Shh!' he soothed, suddenly scooping her up into his arms again to cradle her against his silk-clad chest. 'It can't be that bad.'

'Y-yes, it c-can!' she gasped, fighting for breath as

she buried her wet face on his shoulder. 'He's g-going to take them away. He's g-going to take my b-babies.'

'All right, then, sweetheart. Let it out,' he said in a gentle sing-song as he held her even more tightly and began to rock her. 'Let it all out.' And his voice was as soothing as the hand he used to stroke her hair.

She was vaguely aware that he was now sitting on the settee and that she was cradled on his lap like a little child, but overwhelming all that was the utter relief at being able to let go of all the tension that had been building up inside her for all these years.

Ever since Martin had left she'd been subconsciously dreading this happening. It hadn't been a problem all while he'd been going from one gorgeous young woman to the next, even younger, even more gorgeous one. The fears had escalated when he'd finally married one of them, knowing that he wasn't the sort of man to want to go through the nappies-and-sleepless-nights stage all over again.

Finally the tears began to slow and she had to take stock of where she was. On the man's lap, for heaven's sake. He was a complete stranger and she was wrapped around him, sobbing her heart out on his shoulder.

'You only came to deliver some w-wallpaper,' she hiccuped, desperate for a tissue. 'And you got s-soaked.'

'Twice,' he pointed out huskily, close enough to her ear to stir the damp strands against her temple. 'Once with fresh water and once with salty.'

The hint of laughter she could hear in his voice briefly lifted the corners of her mouth in response but she didn't want to lift her head. It was far too comfortable where it was. Anyway, she needed a hankie and had no idea where—

'Here.' Nick nudged the fingers curled tightly in the silky fabric of his borrowed dressing-gown. She opened her hand and he pressed a handful of tissues into it. 'Mop up first, and then you can tell me what that was all about.'

His matter-of-factness about her red nose and tear-swollen eyes steadied her where open sympathy would have had her cringing in embarrassment.

'I'm sorry,' she muttered. 'You didn't need this on top of everything else. I'll just...'

When she would have scrambled inelegantly off his lap he stopped her by the simple expedient of tightening his arms around her.

'Stay,' he whispered, the sound temptation personified to someone who felt as lonely as Frankie did. The only person to whom she'd been able to unburden herself in the last few years had been Sam, but now that she was married to Daniel...

'Tell me,' he urged, gently thumbing away a stray tear. 'I take it you were talking about your husband?'

'*Ex*-husband,' she reminded him swiftly. 'As of seven years ago.'

'And after seven years he's suddenly decided that he wants custody?'

'Well, he's married again, hasn't he?' she explained, cringing when she heard the bitterness in her voice. She wouldn't want him to misunderstand. 'Not that I begrudge him. He had to grow up some time, I suppose.'

'So, can't his new wife have children? Is that why he's trying for custody?'

She shrugged. 'Don't know.' There was an audible tremor to her indrawn breath. 'There have been a string of women since the divorce...well, before then, except I didn't know about *them*. Anyway, when I heard he was getting married I was so certain that his new wife wasn't going to be interested in children, and I knew he wouldn't want to go through the puppy-training years. He couldn't wait to get away from them the first time round.'

Tears started to well up in her eyes again and she bit her lip to try to subdue them.

'Then, yesterday evening, when he came to collect them for the weekend, he said it was just a courtesy thing, but he was informing me that now he was married, he could provide a better home for Laura and Katie than me, so he would be applying for the custody arrangements to be reversed.' Pain tightened a vicious hand around her heart, making it difficult to speak for a moment. 'It would mean that they would go to live with him. That I would only get to see them for alternate weekends and holidays.'

In spite of her efforts the tears began to fall again, a trickle at first but a flood was imminent.

'What do your daughters think about it?'

His question forced her to concentrate, delaying the inevitable a little while longer.

'I don't know,' she admitted in a strangled whisper. 'They had already left the house to get in the car when he told me what he was going to do, and by the time I recovered from the shock he was already climbing in with them. I suppose he's told them by now.'

'You mean, he didn't even have the courtesy of giving you the chance to be there, in case they were upset and needed their mother?' He gave a snort of derision. 'If that's the way he treats his family, what's he like with his patients?'

'Patients?' Frankie was lost for a moment. 'Martin doesn't have patients, he has clients. He's a lawyer.'

He groaned and shook his head. 'That's called jumping to conclusions, isn't it? I automatically presumed that *he* was Dr Long, and it's you.'

'With me wielding the hose, it didn't really give us a chance for formal introductions. I'm Frances Long, mostly known to her friends as Frankie.'

Irrespective of the fact that she was still cradled on his silk-clad lap, she held out her hand to him.

'Frankie?' He chuckled as he wrapped long fingers warmly around hers. 'I don't believe it.'

'Why not? It's unusual, but it's not that funny.'

His blue eyes were sparkling down at her and the expression in them was doing strange things to her insides and setting all her nerve-endings humming.

'It's only funny if you remember the song,' he explained, reaching up almost absently to smooth a gentle finger over her cheek. 'Because some of my friends used to call me Johnny.'

'Frankie and Johnny.' She rolled her eyes but couldn't help joining in when he started to sing the opening line.

Their voices faded away on the last word of the first line, their eyes suddenly caught with an unbreakable intensity as the sound of it wrapped itself around them.

Lovers...

All of a sudden Frankie realised that this moment had been coming ever since she'd met him. There had been a strange sort of inevitability about it from the moment she'd seen him standing in her garden, soaking wet, and hadn't been able to take her eyes off him.

She'd been the old-fashioned sort of woman who hadn't looked at another man since she'd first gone out with her husband-to-be. The divorce seemed to have completely blunted her appreciation for the male half of the human race until just a short while ago.

For the first time in years she'd met a man and she hadn't been able to control her reaction to him.

The fact that they were alone in her empty house didn't help her sanity, neither did the knowledge that they were both all too aware that she was cradled on his lap and that each of them was wearing just a single garment. She could see it in the flare of blue heat in his eyes that seemed to sear her right to her poor bruised heart.

Her breath caught in her throat when she realised that her nipples were tightening again, this time in response to the predatory look that was darkening his gaze and the tension that was wrapping around them.

'Frankie,' he breathed, his voice sounding almost rusty in the silent room. 'If you don't want me to kiss you…'

Not want him to kiss her? Suddenly that was all she could think about. The sensation of his mouth touching hers, the taste…

'Frankie!' he groaned, and she realised that she'd just run the tip of her tongue over her own lips. 'Yes or no?'

She should say no, for the sake of her peace of mind, but she'd been so lonely for so long, so isolated, even in a crowd. So concerned with taking care of everyone else and taking nothing for herself.

If she said yes…

Just the thought of that mouth settling over hers, forming an intimate connection that needed no words to let them communicate their deepest needs… After seven long years of numb isolation, she only had to look at the man and every nerve in her body craved a deeper contact.

He must have been able to see her answer in her eyes because his head was already swooping down to meet hers as she whispered, 'Yes.'

CHAPTER TWO

SHE should have said no.

That was the last sane thought Frankie had before every notion she'd ever had about kisses disappeared.

This was like nothing she'd ever known. Not just a meeting of mouths but within seconds a sharing of souls.

More.

The only thought in her head was that she wanted more...*needed* more of this man and his kisses. Then, all too soon, she knew they needed more than kisses.

Mouths opened, tongues tangled and explored, hearts raced. Hands stroked then delved and stroked again, clothing all too easily discarded to leave them flesh against flesh.

There was no time for self-consciousness over a body no longer in the first fresh flush of youth, no need for it when he was just as avid, just as greedy to explore, to hold, to give, to take.

The explosion came frighteningly fast, erupting with a brilliant light behind her eyes which only intensified when she felt the answering throb of his release deep inside her.

And even that wasn't enough, neither was their second shared climax under the shower. Only the third, achingly slow and tender when they finally made it as far as her bed, was enough to make her collapse into slumber.

* * *

25

It was dark when Frankie woke surrounded by tangled sheets and it took her a moment to separate dreams from reality.

'Oh, my…' she breathed silently, hardly daring to peer over her shoulder at the other side of the bed.

When she saw it was empty she flopped over onto her back, not sure whether she was more relieved or disappointed that he had gone.

It was one thing to be caught up in an unpremeditated sexual explosion, but it would have been quite another to wake up beside the man and have to make polite conversation while they extricated themselves from the embarrassment of The Morning After.

She groaned aloud. What on earth had possessed her? She'd never done anything like that before, not even with Martin in the first heady days of their marriage, and once the girls had arrived…

She snorted in derision.

After the children had arrived, what sex they'd had had always been limited to an almost silent encounter after the light had been turned out for the night. If it hadn't been so sad she might have found some humour in the fact that it had almost exactly followed the line of the old joke about the deterioration in a marriage— tri-weekly, then try weekly, then try weakly. For them, it had all too rapidly dwindled from a Friday-night routine into something that had been almost a perfunctory bodily function.

Absolutely *nothing* like the searing experience of last night.

Her cheeks heated when she remembered the sounds she had made…*they* had made…at the height of passion. Just thinking about it tightened those intimate muscles deep inside and made her breath hitch in her throat as she felt desire stir again.

What was it about the man that had made her feel more like a woman than she ever had before, stretch marks and all?

She gave a growl of exasperation and scrambled out of the wreck of her bed, knowing that she wasn't going to be able to sleep any more even though it was still pitch dark outside.

An hour later she was still fighting to keep the images inside her head from taking over. She'd stripped the bed and remade it with fresh sheets, refusing to allow herself to bury her face in his pillow to see if she could find a lingering trace of his presence. She'd set the washing-machine going and had even sat down to a proper breakfast, but none of it had worked.

It wasn't as if there was much housework left to do either. She hadn't slept at all on Friday night and then had spent half the day yesterday using frantic activity to try to subdue her fury at Martin's pronouncement. But she certainly couldn't face that wallpaper, much though the job needed doing. All she had to do was look at the carrier bag and she was seeing the drops of water that had run down his clever face and dripped onto the plastic.

It was a very short journey from that image to the one where the two of them had been intimately entwined under the pelting spray of the shower, laughing as they'd licked the drops of water from each other's faces…bodies…

'Dammit! I might as well go in and clear some paperwork!' she exclaimed in disgust when her body began to respond to the mental pictures. The rest of the staff in the practice already knew how hard she found

the empty weekends when Laura and Katie were with
their father, so it shouldn't raise any eyebrows that she
was there on one of her precious days off.

Even if they were to make a comment, she ration-
alised as she set off in an unexpected flurry of snow-
flakes, she had Martin's latest bombshell as a valid
reason for her unrest. She could only thank God that
none of them would ever know what else had happened
to her this weekend. They would probably never believe that she could have done something so out of
character...so potentially dangerous...as to go to bed
with a complete stranger.

The increasingly treacherous journey into the surgery
started with a car filled with the conflicting emotions
of guilt and relief—guilt at what she'd done and relief
that her house was isolated enough that no one would
have known how long her visitor had stayed last night
or what time he'd finally left this morning.

By the time she gingerly slotted her car into one of
the spaces in the staff car park she'd run through the
gamut of emotions, finally working her way to regret—
the realisation that even if a similar opportunity arose,
it wouldn't...*couldn't* happen again.

Making that decision helped to calm her jumping
nerves, as did the prospect of familiar tasks. There was
something very soothing about being in the everyday
surroundings of the staffroom, not least because they
held absolutely no memories of a certain tall, dark and
handsome man who had passed through her life so
spectacularly.

She was sorting through the pile of junk mail which
had accumulated in her pigeonhole by the time her
sense of humour surfaced.

'I wonder... Does that mean I went to bed with a toy boy?' she murmured with a hastily stifled chuckle. Johnny would certainly qualify on several counts, not least the fact that he must be several years younger than she was, indisputably good-looking and apparently completely unencumbered. 'And if one of the requirements is that he should know how to satisfy a woman, he certainly gets full marks from me!'

'What are you muttering about?' demanded Jack Lawrence as he struggled into the room with one hand full of paperwork. The other was clutching the monogrammed medical bag his proud GP father had given him to celebrate the completion of his GP training. 'You're not on duty today, are you?'

'Neither are you,' she retorted smartly. 'And unless your social life has collapsed dramatically, you haven't got the excuse of an empty house to tempt you into doing voluntary overtime.'

'Hey! I resent that!' he exclaimed with an indignant scowl. 'Can I help it if everybody is attracted to my charm and my sweet nature?'

Frankie blew a raspberry. It was probably his looks and his taste in cars, as much as anything, that all the women around went for. 'So, if you're so attractive to everybody, what are you doing here? Wouldn't you rather keep your pride and joy nice and safe in the garage than take it out where someone might skid into it?'

'Of course I would, but, then, I'm such a self-sacrificing sort of person that I've turned out to form the welcoming committee,' he said righteously. 'You remember? Nick Johnson, an old colleague from our training days, is joining the practice. It's worked out well, now that he and Vicky are getting married.'

Frankie remembered. Vicky Lawrence was Jack's younger sister and had returned home to her roots to nurse in Denison Memorial Hospital. Jack had come in for some ribbing when his sister and his old friend Nick had finally become engaged some twelve years after he'd first introduced them. Confirmed-bachelor Jack hadn't been able to understand why they'd suddenly decided to 'get serious' and he had backpedalled rapidly when some members of staff had suggested that it would be his turn next to take the plunge into matrimony.

'I did an on-call swap with Joe for today so that I could spend some time showing Nick around,' Jack was explaining while he measured coffee into the filter with his usual haphazard panache and set the coffee machine going. 'Then we can dump him right in at the deep end tomorrow.'

Frankie winced when she saw how strong the brew was going to be. She could do with another shot of caffeine but that was going to need diluting with a hefty whack of milk and sugar if it wasn't going to corrode her insides.

She turned back to her task, deciding that she'd wait until Jack had taken their new recruit off on a tour of the unit before she helped herself.

She was quite glad, now, that she'd come in today. The new man had been formally interviewed by the three most senior members of the practice and had met most of the others, but for some reason she hadn't seen him before. All she knew was that he and Jack had first met when they'd begun their medical training together in the city, and had kept up the friendship ever since.

She was deep into her perusal of yet another flyer for yet another all-singing, all-dancing drug preparation when there was a brief tap on the door beside her, then it swung open. From her position behind it, she couldn't see who was there but Jack's reaction left her in no doubt.

'You're here!' he exclaimed with a broad grin. 'I was beginning to wonder if the weather was going to frighten you off. Hey, Frankie, come out from behind there and meet my old friend, Nick Johnson. Johnny, this is Frankie Long.' He paused, obviously struck by what he'd just said. 'Hey! How about that? Frankie and Johnny. Do you remember that song?'

Frankie couldn't have answered if her life had depended on it. She was barely able to remember how to breathe, let alone form a coherent sentence, as she stared into disastrously familiar blue eyes.

Of all the people she had expected to see walking into this room, he would have been the last one in the world.

Why hadn't he said something so that she could have been prepared for this? Surely he must have realised that she'd thought he'd been delivering that damned wallpaper because he was somehow connected with the shop? Was he going to say something to Jack?

Her heart was pounding with dread, the sound of it almost deafening as she forced herself to hold the man's gaze.

He was smiling at her, his blue eyes very clear and focused, and suddenly she somehow knew that he was going to keep their secret.

'Don't be an idiot, Jack,' he chided easily. 'Of course Frankie and I have met. You left a message at Reception yesterday, telling me to go and collect the mobile phone and paperwork from her house, and a map showing me how to get there.' He held up the

items in question and it was the first Frankie had realised that they had even disappeared from the table in
her hallway.

She managed a weak answering smile, but it wasn't
until her brain started to work logically again that she
realised that she had nothing to fear from this man.

He hadn't been caught on the hop with the introduction because he'd already known who she was. Be-
sides, if Johnny, her incomparable lover of last night,
was also Nick Johnson, new GP in the practice, he was
engaged to Jack's sister and would have just as much
reason to keep their brief encounter quiet as she did.

Her relief that her disastrous lapse in propriety
wasn't going to have repercussions was enormous, so
much so that for a moment it overwhelmed everything
else. It was only when the two men had left to take
their tour around the building that other emotions began to surface.

The first was a crashing sense of disillusionment that
such an attractive man should have waited so long to
pledge himself to a woman—they'd known each other
for twelve years, for heaven's sake—and before they
even made their way up the aisle, he was willing to
cheat on her. Were all men just like Martin under the
skin? Were none of them prepared to be faithful?

The fact that he had been the most sensitive, caring,
passionate lover she'd ever known became much less
attractive when she realised that she must just be one
among many on whom he'd practised his wiles.

With the shine well and truly taken off her memories,
her home had seemed a far less threatening place than
the practice. The last thing Frankie needed was to
spend any more time in Nick's presence until she'd got

her scrambled emotions under control. There was also the prospect that Martin might need to drop the girls off early if the condition of the roads became any worse.

In the end, she'd opted to do the dreaded wallpapering and had taken a savage delight in stripping the walls in her bedroom while she planned how she was going to rearrange the furniture.

'By the time I've finished in here, there won't be a single thing to remind me of my stupidity,' she vowed as she scrubbed the denuded walls clean, wishing wryly that she could scrub her memory, too.

The paint around the windows was still too wet to allow her to hang the curtains but, apart from that, the whole room was finished by the time she heard Martin's car draw up outside the house.

She watched Laura and Katie climb out and knew instantly that Martin had told them of his plans. She could see immediately that these weren't the same lively chattering girls who had left two days ago but what she didn't know was what they felt about his plans.

Tears prickled the back of her eyes when she realised just how skewed her priorities had become since she'd last seen her precious daughters. What sort of a mother was she? She should have been worrying about how they would cope with the turmoil looming on the horizon, with the possibility that they might soon be going to live with their father and his new wife. Instead, she'd been falling into bed with a complete stranger and then obsessing about her ability to work with the man on a daily basis.

*   *   *

Monday morning arrived far too soon for Frankie's peace of mind even though she couldn't wait for the disastrous weekend to be over.

She still hadn't managed to have a decent night's sleep—that made three in a row—and the sullen mood Laura had brought back from her visit with her father hadn't improved overnight either. Even Katie was more subdued than usual, her natural bounce completely absent at breakfast.

Without making too much of it, Frankie had tried to find out what Martin had said to them, but neither was forthcoming beyond the bald statement from Laura that he was redecorating their bedrooms ready for when they moved in.

Frankie was still silently cursing her ex-husband's lack of sensitivity in breaking his intentions to them without her input when she dropped the girls off at school, and was mentally composing a blistering diatribe, which she'd probably never have the chance to deliver, all the way to the hospital.

The car park was chaotic, with far too many people taking advantage of the fact that the parking bay markings were covered in snow to park wherever would afford them the least trek through the treacherous stuff.

There had been several inches of it in her driveway at home and she suddenly realised that neither Katie nor Laura had bothered to do so much as make a snowball out of the tempting layer. If she needed anything to tell her how much the new situation was affecting them, that was the proof. And she had absolutely no idea how to persuade them to talk to her.

At nine and eleven, they were growing faster than Japanese knotweed and even though she'd taken care of them for most of their young lives, she suddenly realised that she didn't even know if they were secretly *glad* that they were going to be living with their father soon. After all, she was a busy GP. There wasn't nearly enough time for her to do all the things with them that Martin's stay-at-home wife would.

The phone rang in the staffroom, dragging her out of her self-condemnation with the short buzz that told her it was an internal call.

'Oh, hello, Dr Long,' said Jane Pelly, youngest of the three practice receptionists. 'I didn't know you'd arrived yet. Is Dr Lawrence there?'

'Sorry, Jane. It's just me and the never-ending piles of paperwork. Perhaps he's been delayed by the state of the roads.'

'Drat!' the young woman muttered, already sounding frazzled in spite of the relatively early hour.

'Anything I can do to help?' Frankie offered rashly, suddenly feeling the need to see something other than the usual run of winter coughs and colds to jump-start her day.

'I'm actually trying to track down the new man, Dr Johnson,' Jane explained, sending Frankie's stomach into a slow roll. 'I know he's a friend of Dr Lawrence's and I was hoping he'd know how I could get in contact in a hurry.'

'Problem?' In spite of her reaction to the man's name, there was something in the tone of Jane's voice that was tightening her nerves with a different tension.

'One of the school buses has skidded and crashed. He's down as an A and E specialist, and we're going to need him.'

'Have you got the number of the spare mobile phone?' Frankie suggested. 'I believe Jack organised for him to take it home with him yesterday.'

'Fantastic!' Jane exclaimed fervently. 'I'll try it. In

the meantime, if you've got a few minutes free to take a look at the collection of walking wounded...'

'You tell me,' Frankie countered, her pulse already picking up as the surge of adrenaline kicked in. 'What time is my first patient due and what are the chances they'll be able to get here?'

There was a brief pause while Jane consulted the list. 'Not due for another fifteen or twenty minutes and they'll probably be held up at the crash site as they'll be coming in that way. If you could cover until I find out whether Dr Johnson's on his way...'

That was one of the advantages of working in a small place like Edenthwaite, Frankie thought as she hurried towards their small A and E department. Everyone knew so much about everyone else that the receptionist even knew which road the patient would be travelling to come for their appointment.

Her pulse gave a totally unnecessary skip at the prospect of seeing Johnny...*Nick*, she reminded herself fiercely...in a little while and she sternly ordered it to behave.

She knew only too well that there was a downside to such rural communities—gossip grew faster than staphylococcal infections and was even harder to control. If even one person were to catch a hint of anything untoward between the two of them, they would never hear the end of the speculation.

Unfortunately, she knew that it was one thing to make rational intelligent decisions but it might be entirely another to try to stop herself reacting to the wretched man's presence. But she was going to do her best.

Everything went well when she arrived in Denison Memorial's A and E department. It was full of the purposeful flurry of preparations that would always precede a sudden influx of accident victims, but for the moment there were people already waiting for attention, totally unconnected with the bus crash. If she directed her efforts, she could probably clear most of them before the injured children arrived. At least she could warn the less urgent cases that there might be a long delay before they would be seen.

'Oh, Frankie! Thank goodness!' Mark Fletcher exclaimed when he caught sight of her and beckoned her over.

It was the first time she'd ever seen the hospital manager looking anything but perfectly composed and the only place safe to stand was in the doorway of the sluice.

'Are you seeing patients this morning or are you free?' He ran one hand over his neatly trimmed hair but it wasn't enough to subdue the uncharacteristic disarray.

'I've got a list booked,' she confirmed. 'But I came in early this morning.' She came in early most mornings as she had to drop the girls off at school on the way, but he didn't need to know that.

'Well, how long can you give us in here? The emergency services seem to be revising the number of injuries upwards every time we speak to them. Jack Lawrence is on his way in but we still haven't been able to get hold of Dr Johnson.'

Ruthlessly subduing any stray concern about the man's whereabouts, Frankie thought for a second.

'I'm quite happy to stay until I'm not needed any more, but you'll need to clear it with the rest of the doctors on duty this morning to see if they can cover for me. Is there anyone coming in from the other practices?'

The hospital was at the centre of a fairly wide circle of villages and towns of various sizes, and was able to call on the various GP practices for extra cover in the case of emergencies.

'Several willing, but having difficulties getting here because of the state of the roads,' he supplied succinctly. 'If you could get stuck in, I'll have a word over in the GP unit to see how long they can let you stay on here.'

He whirled and strode away, his brisk steps clear evidence of his former military experience.

'Hey, Frankie. Ready for the fray?' Vicky Lawrence asked, coming into the room as she washed her hands.

'No babies to deliver?' Frankie kept the question light but she couldn't help the flood of guilt that tied her stomach in knots. She'd completely forgotten that she might have to face Nick's fiancée at some stage.

'Not at the moment, so I'm on loan. Any idea what we've got here?'

'From what I caught sight of on the main board, assorted lacerations, foreign bodies and trapped appendages. None of it desperately serious but all of it needing attention. Shall we?' She pulled the neck loop of a plastic apron over her head and gestured towards the main reception area.

Over the last few years she'd done her share of duty in the A and E department but this was the first time she could remember feeling under pressure.

Mark Fletcher had been right about the escalating numbers being reported from the crash site but as she systematically went about the debridement and suturing of the various wounds waiting for her, and removing small components of toys from ears and noses, her overwhelming anxiety was for Nick Johnson.

She knew he was no concern of hers and that there were badly injured patients due at any moment, but all she could think about was what had happened to him. He should have arrived at the surgery ages ago, ready to start his first official day as a member of staff, but there was no sign of him.

Had he had an accident himself? He wouldn't know the roads around here yet. He might not have realised just how treacherous they could be, with black ice forming where natural springs and streams encroached on the roads. Was he, even now, lying broken and bleeding in a heap at the bottom of some scree slope?

And she couldn't even ask, she realised as she passed yet another carefully repaired injury over to be covered with a protective dressing.

With Vicky working just yards away, how would it look if *she* were the one to show concern for such a new colleague? Not good, she admitted as she pierced a hole through a nail to release the pressure of blood collecting underneath it after the digit in question had been firmly slammed in a car door.

Even the patient's squeal of dismay when she saw what was happening wasn't enough to stop Frankie's mind from racing around in circles.

The sound of rapidly approaching sirens only served to tighten the knots in her nerves and she marvelled that her hands remained perfectly steady while she positioned the edges of a scalp wound for supergluing together.

Between them, she and the rest of the staff in A and E had completely cleared the department of waiting patients by the time the first accident victims arrived.

Jack had been with them at the site, so they had already been triaged on site and prioritised according to severity.

'Air ambulance is ferrying the really bad stuff straight to the city,' he told her as he stripped off a decidedly wet padded jacket and dumped it on the back of a chair. 'One of the farmers had to put some sort of scraper attachment on the front of his tractor to clear the road so that the ambulances could get through, otherwise you'd have had some of the less injured here before now.'

'So, how many are we getting here?' She was keeping one eye on the trolleys coming in, two from each vehicle, and the wheelchairs transporting those too shocked to make it to a cubicle under their own steam. It would take a moment for the nursing team to get them settled.

'At least a dozen. Maybe more,' he said grimly as he pulled on an apron. 'Johnny had to go in the city ambulance.'

Her heart leapt up into her throat then dived towards her feet. Johnny…*Nick* had to go in the…

'Why?' she gasped as her imagination ran riot, supplying gruesome images of everything from multiple traumas to death. *No!* something inside her screamed. He was too full of life to…

'It was either that, or perform an amputation at the side of the road,' Jack said, jerking her out of her preoccupation.

'Amputation?' she echoed numbly, wondering how badly his perfect body had been damaged.

'Poor kid was trapped,' Jack explained with a grimace. 'But there's still a chance that his leg might be saved so…'

'Poor kid,' Frankie breathed, her knees as limp as overcooked noodles as everything suddenly became clear. It was one of the pupils who had been injured and Nick had gone with him on the journey to the specialist orthopaedic unit in the nearby city hospital.

Over the next couple of hours, as she patched and mended, splinted, plastered and stitched, she heard far more detail than she ever needed to know about the events of that morning. About the inexperienced car driver apparently growing impatient with the bus driver's caution as he manoeuvred his unwieldy vehicle full of schoolchildren along the twisty road towards Edenthwaite. About the teenager's reckless decision to overtake and his belated panic when he hit ice and lost control. About the fact that not only had he lost his own life, but that he could have destroyed the lives of dozens of children.

And finally, in unending glowing detail, about the doctor who had climbed down the rock-strewn hillside and right inside the shattered bus to help the injured to safety, staying to talk to the trapped boy until he was finally released.

Reading between the lines, Frankie knew that Nick would have been doing far more than keeping his young patient company. She could only imagine how much fluid he would have been pumping into the injured body to prevent the boy's system from shutting down. She could imagine his concern over the prospect of having to take the desperate step of amputating an otherwise healthy limb to save the child's life, and the gamble he'd taken in waiting for a transfer to the orthopaedic unit.

By mid-morning, the worst was over.

Several of the students had needed to stay in for

further treatment, a few would merely need to be under observation overnight, but the majority had been released after treatment to go home with their parents.

There were still the last few minor injuries to be seen to, including the usual head-count of older patients waiting for X-rays after a fall in the snow, when Frankie heard the doors to the A and E department slide open yet again.

She wasn't certain what she'd been expecting, but it was the sudden flood of emotion she felt when she saw Nick striding into the unit that told her she was in serious trouble.

CHAPTER THREE

THE doors slid closed behind Nick, shutting out the miserable cold, but his eyes were already scanning the faces turned towards him.

Why was it that of all of them, the first eyes he met were Frankie's? And why was it that he felt some sort of strange connection between them?

'Nick!' he saw her say, the corners of her mouth curving sweetly when she saw him.

'Johnny!' Vicky exclaimed, and he knew she was hurrying towards him. Guilt hit him hard and fast but still he couldn't drag his gaze away from the bright gleam in eyes the colour of sun-warmed honey.

There was concern in them, and the realisation that Frankie had been worried about him caused more of a kick than the feel of Vicky's hands wrapped around his arm.

'What an introduction to Edenthwaite!' Vicky was saying as she pulled him towards the knot of staff winding down from the worst of the emergency with steaming mugs of tea and coffee. 'You're going to wish you hadn't come here.'

'No chance of that,' Nick said quietly as he paused in front of Frankie. Actually, he hadn't been able to make himself walk past her, in spite of the fact that Vicky was still holding onto his arm. 'Sorry to leave you in the lurch.'

'Unavoidable circumstances,' she murmured, and he was entranced to see the soft wash of colour spread over her cheeks. Was she finding it equally hard not to react to him? Was there a double meaning in her words?

'How did it go with that lad?' someone called, and he finally managed to tear his eyes away from her. This was neither the time nor the place to ponder the strange attraction that had flared between the two of them, nor the guilt and remorse that struck him anew when he saw the open trust in Vicky's face.

'His leg was a mess and he's having some micro-surgery done while we speak, but there was no apparent nerve damage and they're hopeful that they can repair the circulation to his foot.'

There was a concerted sigh of relief and he suddenly realised that most of the people in the department either knew the child in question or at least a member of his family. It was just another facet of his new job that he was going to have to get used to.

'Well,' Vicky said pertly, gazing up at him out of guileless blue eyes framed by wisps of baby-fine blonde hair, 'while you've been jaunting around the countryside, having free scenic tours, we've been mucking in and doing all the hard work. And I thought it was the chance to do A and E work, as well as general practice, that attracted you to Edenthwaite?'

'Must have been another attraction here,' someone teased, then chuckled when Vicky blushed.

Guilt swamped him again when he remembered how he had betrayed this beautiful young woman's trust. Vicky was his fiancée, he reminded himself, but still he couldn't stop himself looking away from her to search out Frankie's eyes.

The answering guilt and pain he saw in their depths was a shock almost as vicious as a blow, and he had to watch in silence as she whirled away to hurry out of the room.

For the next few minutes he had to endure the back-slapping and congratulations of his new colleagues as Vicky completed the introductions. He hoped he was smiling and making all the right responses, but all the while he knew that he was going to have to search Frankie out. Something inside him, some spark of the decency that still remained in spite of all evidence to the contrary, was telling him that they needed to speak about what had happened between them.

What on earth had possessed him?

He'd barely been in the area for more than an hour and he'd ended up taking one of his new colleagues to bed. He'd never done anything remotely like it before, even in those distant days when he'd had more testosterone than common sense.

It wasn't enough of an excuse to say that she was a gorgeous woman, or that she was someone who sparked something deep inside him that he'd never felt before. He had asked Vicky to marry him and had fully intended to be a faithful husband, but there was something… Was it something in him, or in Frankie, or in the combination of the two of them, that had made them throw prudence to the winds?

That combination had certainly been combustible. The two of them together had been far more explosive than any situation he'd ever encountered before and the shock waves were still echoing through him.

As was the guilt.

Not only was he feeling guilty for betraying Vicky's trust, but there was also a black dread deep inside that he might have taken advantage of Frankie's shaky emotional state in the wake of her ex-husband's threat.

'Hey, Vicky!' someone called, holding the phone up towards her. 'A call from the ward to say there's one on the way in. Woman in labour with contractions coming about four minutes apart. Should be here in about twenty minutes, given a clear road. She's already spoken to her midwife.'

Vicky squeezed his arm as she reached up to deliver a hasty kiss. 'Nick, I must go and make sure everything's ready. Come up and visit if you get a chance, to see how the rest of the world goes about this medical stuff. We can't all be doing the heroic things like climbing down hillsides and into crashed buses.'

Nick watched her walking out of the room, her willowy body slim and trim in the navy trousers and mid-blue tunic combination she wore as her uniform. She'd been an enchanting child of fourteen when he'd first met her, all long legs, flyaway blonde hair and baby-blue eyes. She had developed into a wonderful young woman over the last twelve years, someone he was proud to be marrying, but...

He sighed heavily as he made his way from the A and E department, passing through the central reception area on his way to the GP unit in the east wing.

That was probably part of the problem. He'd known Vicky since she was fourteen and he had known even then that she had developed a massive crush on him.

Over the years, he'd expected her girlish passions to find another target, probably a whole series of them before she settled on the man she would eventually marry.

Except it hadn't happened.

It didn't seem to matter that his visits had been few and far between or even that he'd eventually become involved in a long-term relationship that had seemed destined to end in his own marriage. Whenever they'd met, she'd gazed at him out of those innocent blue eyes and he'd known that she'd still been harbouring her impossible dream.

Then his own life had taken a decidedly uncomfortable turn and he'd realised that he wasn't quite the judge of character that he'd thought, and Vicky was still there, her smile telling him that she still believed in him.

That belief had helped him to make some unexpected changes in the direction of his career, and now he found himself engaged and starting his first job as a fully qualified GP.

Except, within hours of arriving in Edenthwaite, it looked as if he had already ruined everything.

Already, he had noticed changes in himself. First, there was his preoccupation with watching Frankie whenever she was in the vicinity, then there was the fact that he seemed to have spent an inordinate amount of time since he'd left her sleeping in her bed wishing that he had the right to join her there again.

Then, just a few moments ago, Vicky had reached up to kiss him and without a second thought he'd turned his head away so her lips had brushed his cheek. If that were to continue, how long would it be before she noticed and wondered what was going on?

He needed to speak to Frankie.

The two of them needed to sit down together and speak about what had happened. Perhaps then he would be able to relegate those mind-blowing events to the past, where they belonged.

*　　*　　*

'I am *not* hiding,' Frankie muttered through clenched teeth as she tried vainly to make sense of the instructions on the computer screen.

The sensation of connection that she'd felt when her eyes had met Nick's was nothing important. Just a by-product of the fact that she'd spilled her troubles on his shoulder the other night.

He was engaged to marry Vicky, who had every right to stand there with her hands wrapped around his arm. The sharp pain she'd felt around her heart was nothing more than hunger pangs or...or stress or...

'Blast it!' The screen had gone totally blank now, and she had absolutely no idea what she'd done.

Exasperation tempted her to switch the thing off, but she really wanted to know how many of her over-fifty ladies hadn't yet been for breast screening. It was pride as much as anything that made her persevere. She didn't know whether it was something to do with the fact that she was a female GP, but last time she'd checked the figures she'd had a higher percentage of compliance than any of the other GPs in the practice.

Not that she needed the information at this precise minute, but if she kept busy she wouldn't have to admit that she was staying out of Nick's way.

The phone rang and she reached for the receiver without even looking at it.

'Frankie?'

She didn't know how she knew that it was Nick's voice when she'd never heard it over the phone before but the instant shiver of awareness caught her by surprise.

'Speaking.'

Her brusque reply seemed to have silenced him, but she was incapable of saying anything more. What *was* it about the man that he should have such an effect on her?

'Nick Johnson here. Are you busy?'

That surprised a brief chuckle out of her.

'You ask if a GP is busy! It's obvious that you're a new boy,' she mocked.

In the silence she replayed her own words and cringed. There was nothing like putting her feet in her mouth with both hands. She knew only too well that he was younger by several years, but to have called him a boy…

'We need to talk,' he said gruffly. 'When would be good for you?'

Never, the voice inside her head screamed. It was bad enough, after their explosive intimacy, to have to see him around the practice. The idea of keeping her reaction towards him to herself in a one-to-one situation was something else entirely.

'Frankie?' The touch of impatience in his voice told her he wasn't happy to be left hanging on.

She glanced at her watch and realised with a shock just how much time she'd spent incarcerated in her room.

'I don't know,' she said distractedly, exiting the program she'd been trying to access and switching off the computer. 'It's time I was leaving to pick the girls up from school, and tomorrow's going to be a full day, especially if the weather doesn't improve overnight, and—'

'Fine,' he interrupted brusquely, and she heard a hint of steel entering his voice for the first time since she'd met him. 'I get the point. You're a very busy person. But, Frankie, make no mistake. Sooner or later, we *are* going to talk.'

Before she had time to think of a reply, let alone voice one, she found herself holding a dead phone.

'Ouch!' She gingerly put the receiver down, almost expecting it to explode. That had definitely been a man who seemed to like getting his own way. There was obviously more to him than good looks and a superb bedside manner.

She stifled a giggle when her subconscious presented her with a picture of a totally gorgeously naked Nick Johnson making house calls.

'Enough of that! Go and get your kids!' she scolded herself, quite shocked that she should even have thought of such a thing. Her imagination had never been that raunchy before she'd met that man.

'Oh, Dr Long. Thank goodness you haven't gone,' Mara Frost said almost as soon as she reached the reception area. 'Mrs Vidler is on her way in with Pam. Apparently she can't keep anything down and her stomach is very sore. She should be here in about ten minutes.'

'Who's being sick? Pam or Mrs Vidler?' Pam must be about seven now, and Mrs Vidler was almost eight months pregnant with a much-longed-for second child.

'Mrs Vidler. And she's terrified it means there's something wrong with the baby. She specifically asked if you were here.'

Frankie could well imagine. Complications after her first baby was born had made this child almost a miracle. Supervising the long course of treatment and monitoring the resulting pregnancy had meant that she'd built up a closer than usual relationship with the young woman.

She flicked another glance at her watch and groaned.

The bell would be ringing at any moment to signal the end of lessons.

'Laura and Katie will be waiting for me. Is there anyone going that way who could pick them up and bring them here to wait?'

'Daniel's already left to get his two—' Mara began, only to be interrupted.

'I can get them,' offered a voice behind her, and she nearly groaned again.

'No one knows you, so the school wouldn't release them to you,' she pointed out with a crazy sense of relief. 'It's a safety precaution, so no one can snatch children.'

'So you'll need to phone the school to tell them I'm coming, and then give me a note to confirm I'm who I say I am,' he said logically, already reaching for his keys.

'But—'

'That will certainly solve the problem,' Mara jumped in, and slid a piece of the surgery's headed notepaper across the desk towards Frankie. 'I can keep an eye on them until you're finished with Mrs Vidler. I'll be looking after her Pam anyway.'

Frankie gave in with good grace, quickly writing a note confirming that Dr Nick Johnson had her permission to pick Laura and Katie up as she'd been unavoidably detained.

'You'd better give Dr Johnson a photo of the girls,' Mara suggested as she straightened up from her task.

'Why?'

'Extra identification, and so that you'll recognise them,' she explained with a smile for Nick.

'Oh, but—' Frankie began, her mouth almost getting

ahead of her brain until she caught the quick shake of his head.

But he's already seen a photo of them, she'd been about to say, and wouldn't *that* have given people something to get their teeth into? As far as anyone else knew, Nick had merely turned up at her house yesterday to pick up the mobile phone and some paperwork. Hopefully no one would ever know exactly how much time he'd spent with her and what they'd done during that time.

Silently she fished her purse out of the depths of her handbag and extracted the photo that always travelled with her wherever she went.

'Pretty girls,' he said with a smile as he looked at the picture that was almost the twin of the one on the notice-board in her kitchen, then met Frankie's wary eyes. 'They obviously take after their mother.'

'Do you want me to get the school on the phone?' Mara prompted, breaking the current of awareness that had begun to flow between them again.

It didn't take long to explain the situation to the school secretary—it wasn't the first time such a situation had arisen with one member of staff or another— but all the parents felt happier knowing that the security system was in place.

Frankie was exasperated to find her eyes following Nick as he left the reception area, and she had to force herself to turn away.

'Send Mrs Vidler straight through as soon as she gets here,' she said, setting one foot firmly in front of the other on her way to her room. It felt very strange thinking that Nick, the man she'd shared her bed and her body with, was on his way to collect her daughters from school. The fact that she had a sudden insane wish that the three of them would take to each other was just one more guilt trip to add to the mounting tally. All she could do was try to concentrate on the possible complications that were bringing Marian Vidler here in such a panic.

'I'm sorry,' the young woman began as soon as she reached the door. 'I know you're supposed to be getting your kids from school. I've had Pam home all day because we couldn't get out of the lane this morning.'

'Don't worry about it,' Frankie soothed. 'One of the other doctors is collecting them. Now, come over here and sit down. Tell me what's wrong.'

Marian took a step forward then suddenly stopped, and Frankie saw a strange expression spreading over her face.

'Oh!' she exclaimed in panic. 'Oh, no!'

She didn't need to say anything more. The rapidly spreading puddle between her feet was enough to tell Frankie what was happening.

'I think we need to get you to a midwife,' Frankie said as she leapt to her feet to hurry to her patient's side.

'No! It's too soon!' she moaned, feebly fighting the supporting arm Frankie tried to wrap around her shoulders. 'It's not due to come for weeks yet.'

'I think Junior Vidler has other ideas about that,' Frankie teased gently while she did some mental calculations.

Was it four weeks early, or closer to three? Either way, they were going to have to make the best of it because labour-delaying drugs weren't an option. With her waters gone, so was the baby's barrier against *in utero* infection. There was no choice now but to deliver the baby as quickly and as safely as possible.

'Come and sit down for a minute while I make some calls,' she urged as she draped a towel over the mock-leather seat of a nearby chair and helped the young woman to lower her less than agile frame onto it.

A quick call across to the little maternity department over in the hospital's north wing was enough to confirm that Faith, the midwife, would meet them when they arrived. Then it was just a case of alerting the practice receptionist to what was going on and instructing her to grab the nearest wheelchair.

'What about Pam?' Marian Vidler gasped as Jane appeared with a purloined wheelchair sporting the word Physio stencilled across the back. 'And my husband. He doesn't know that the baby's coming,' she added, her face screwed up with the sudden onset of pain.

'We can take care of all that. Trust us,' Jane promised, standing by as Frankie waited for the pain to ebb then helping her into the chair. 'All you have to do is concentrate on bringing this little one into the world. I've got your phone number on my computer and I'll call him as soon as I get back to my desk.'

'And Pam?'

'At the moment, she's busy feeding the fish for me, so I'd better get back before she gives them enough for a month.'

'Happy now?' Frankie asked, hoping she sounded more relaxed than she felt. She was torn between wanting to deliver the young woman into expert hands as soon as possible and needing her to be calm. As yet she had no idea why labour had started so early, or why Marian had been so sick. If there was something wrong, the sooner it was discovered the better, and there she saw no point in delaying down here to do things like blood-pressure checks when they were only going to be repeated as soon as they arrived at the other end of the building.

'I'm scared,' Marian admitted in a shaky voice, suddenly sounding close to tears. 'I don't know what I'd do if anything happened to this baby.'

She laid protective hands over her prominent bump and Frankie could remember just how she felt. She'd had those same feelings with both of her pregnancies, but had put it down to the fact that she'd known far too much for her own peace of mind about all the things that could go wrong.

'Couldn't wait to see us, could you?' Faith quipped with a cheerful smile when the lift doors opened, the hint of her Irish accent giving the words a musical lilt. 'Or was it the babe you're in a hurry to meet?'

'I don't seem to have any say in the matter,' Marian Vidler grumbled into the brief gap between the sudden onset of fierce contractions. She'd had two just in the time it had taken to travel from the GP unit to the other side of Denison Memorial.

'Ow!' she whimpered, signalling the onset of a third and Frankie glanced quickly at her watch.

'How quickly?' Faith demanded briskly, obviously alerted by something in Frankie's expression.

'Three minutes and accelerating rapidly,' the GP supplied, letting her know that they needed to move quickly.

'Evidently, this isn't going to be any sort of leisurely delivery,' Faith commented with a practised smile to hide her sudden concern. 'Let's get you in here and take a look.'

Frankie had stepped back to allow the midwife to take over when her hand was seized in a fierce grip.

'Come with me,' Marian begged. 'Please!'

Frankie glanced up at Faith who nodded swiftly.

'I don't mind having extra assistance,' she agreed cheerfully as she lent a steadying hand while the young woman perched uncomfortably on the edge of the table. 'I can get them to do all the boring stuff so I get to do the exciting things—like get my hands on the babe.'

'I can take a hint,' Frankie retorted, glad to see that their banter was helping her patient to relax. 'I get to do the fetching and carrying while you get all the glory.'

'Exactly so!' Faith exclaimed, snapping a pair of sterile gloves on and reaching into the delivery kit while Frankie helped their charge out of her wet clothing.

She refused to think of other wet clothing and the lean muscular body it had covered, concentrating on wrapping a warm blanket around Marian's shoulders in place of the gown she didn't have time to don.

This time, the contraction made her groan heavily. 'I need to push,' she exclaimed through gritted teeth.

'Not yet, sweetheart, please!' Faith demanded sharply enough to grab her patient's attention. 'Pant a moment while I take a look. We don't want you doing the babe a mischief because the door isn't open wide enough.'

Marian groaned again, wild-eyed, but she managed to comply.

'Dear Lord, you are in a hurry!' Faith exclaimed as she made her examination. 'I can almost shake hands with the babe already!'

Marian was startled into a huff of laughter.

'Does that mean I can push? *Please?*'

'As soon as you like,' Faith confirmed as she straightened up. 'You're fully dilated and ready to go.'

'Thank God for that,' she moaned, clearly feeling the start of the next contraction.

There was hardly time for any of them to breathe over the next ten minutes, Frankie taking over the task of monitoring Marian's elevated blood pressure and acting as her cheering squad while Faith concentrated on the other end of the job.

In an almost frighteningly fast time they were watching the emergence of a head crowned with thick dark hair, swiftly followed by a slippery body and surprisingly long limbs.

'It's a boy, Marian,' Frankie said with sudden tears in her eyes, not caring that her hand had nearly gone numb in her patient's tight grip. 'You've got a son.'

'And he's a real beauty,' Faith added as she checked him over then wrapped him in the waiting blanket with the speed and efficiency born of much practice. 'Not a bad size in spite of the fact he was in a hurry to get here,' she went on with a twinkle in her eye as she placed him in his mother's arms.

'I'm just glad you decided to come in when you did, or Pam might have ended up having to deliver her brother at the side of the road,' Frankie managed to say, fighting the ridiculous tears that burned behind her eyes.

This was such a special moment with each new baby. One that she hadn't forgotten in spite of the fact that her girls were now nine and eleven.

Suddenly she was swamped by desolation at the knowledge that she'd never know that magic again— that instant when a new life born of her body was placed in her hands and her heart reached out to it to enfold it for ever.

It had happened with both Laura and Katie, and

she'd known that from that moment she would protect them with the ferocity of a mother lion with her cubs.

The knock on the door behind her dragged her out of her thoughts. It announced the arrival of Marian's husband and reminded her that it was long past time that she went to retrieve her children from Jane's supervision.

She promised that Pam would be escorted up to be introduced to her baby brother but there were more personal thoughts whirling furiously through her head.

She had carried her two babies, nurturing them inside her body until they were ready to be born, and had continued to care for them the best she could for the last eleven years. The commitment she'd felt towards them in that first moment that they'd been placed in her arms hadn't dimmed one iota in spite of the time that had passed. They were her babies to love and protect and they would still be her babies even when they were old enough to have babies of their own.

And Martin thought she would calmly stand by while he took them away from her? No way!

He might be a successful lawyer, but there were some things that were more important to young girls on the brink of womanhood than the legal niceties of a newly established two-parent unit. While they were going through the traumas and upheavals of puberty and adolescence, they needed the security of knowing that the parent they lived with had never wavered in her commitment to love them and care for them.

By the time she reached the reception area that served the GP unit she could feel a new resolve in her step.

She was going to fight.

Just because Martin was a lawyer, that didn't mean

that he automatically *had* to win. The fact that she'd cared for Laura and Katie since they were born—and single-handedly for the last seven years—*and* the fact that they were growing up normal, happy, healthy children must surely count for something when such decisions were being made.

Then she stepped round the corner towards the lines of chairs in the waiting area and came to a complete halt, her breath halted in her throat.

Whatever she'd expected when Nick had volunteered to collect Laura and Katie from school it hadn't been that he would still be sitting with them nearly an hour later. And it *certainly* hadn't been that Katie would be sitting beside him while he read to her out of one of the books from the children's corner, or that Laura—watchful, newly moody Laura—would be laughing out loud at whatever it was that Nick had just said.

Something inside clenched tight around her heart. *This* was what had been missing from her girls' lives, and it wasn't something they'd had from their father even when the two of them had been married.

Sadness washed over her in an icy deluge at the realisation. It was one thing to finally understand what had been missing from their lives and to know that Martin was never going to be the one to give it to them.

It was another thing entirely to realise that the man who could have given it to them was promised to another woman.

CHAPTER FOUR

'MUMMY!' Katie sang out as she caught sight of her. 'Come and listen. Nick is telling us a 'tically correct story and it's ever so funny.'

'*Politically* correct,' Laura amended with all the disdain of an older sister, then couldn't help grinning in turn. 'You know, where everyone has to say "chairperson" or "postperson" instead of "chairman" or "postman" and the princess gets arrested for kissing the frog without his permission. Come and listen, Mum. Nick won't mind, will you?'

She turned to him with shining eyes as she made her appeal but he didn't notice. His eyes were already fixed in Frankie's direction, their searing intensity a strange mixture of anger and compassion that she couldn't decipher.

All she knew was that it made her feel things that she shouldn't, deep inside where she hid her most intimate secrets.

'Girls, it's time we were going,' she managed in a rusty voice before she managed to drag her eyes away from his. 'You shouldn't have made Nick...*Dr Johnson*,' she corrected herself firmly, 'stay here with you. He has other things to do.'

'But, Mum...'

'He *said* we could...'

As usual, they both began to speak at once, their words emerging as a hopeless muddle.

'They didn't make me—I volunteered,' Nick inter-

60

rupted quietly, his deeper, almost baritone voice easily overriding their lighter trebles. 'And I didn't have anything better to do.'

'He hasn't even got anything to eat for tea,' Katie informed her importantly. 'I said he could come and share our casserold but he said you hadn't invited him, but you will, won't you, 'cos there's always lots left over so he could eat it.'

'*Casserole*,' Laura corrected with an air of long-suffering while Frankie stood lost for words.

What was she supposed to say now? What *could* she say, especially with Jane standing there with her ears flapping?

To put him off would seem the height of churlishness, especially when he'd been kind enough to collect them from school, to say nothing of entertaining them like this. But to confirm the invitation was equally impossible. He was an engaged man, for heaven's sake. If he needed feeding, Vicky should be the one doing it.

Or was that just her guilty conscience speaking?

She'd done something far worse than feed the man, for heaven's sake. Where was the harm in inviting him to eat with them? It was hardly champagne and oysters, and a plateful of casserole was little enough recompense for his time and trouble.

'Vicky's working late,' he offered quietly, and she couldn't disguise the jolt of surprise that he'd apparently read her mind or the flash of unreasonable jealousy that he was obviously spending time with his beautiful fiancée outside the hospital.

When Katie shifted impatiently on her seat she also realised that she'd been hovering indecisively for far too long.

'So you're not above Jack's bachelor trick of mooching a meal,' she teased.

'Home-cooked beats take-away hands down,' he confirmed, then turned to grin at Katie. 'Especially when I've been reliably informed that it's been cooking for a million hours.'

'And afterwards he could tell us some more of that story,' Katie added with an excited little bounce.

'Please, Mummy?' Lauren added with a persuasive smile.

'Please, Mummy,' Nick added as an echo, making them all laugh.

It was so good to see the two of them smiling again that she couldn't find it in her heart to refuse.

It didn't matter that she knew only too well that having the man in her house again was the last thing she needed. It was already far too hard to go into any of the rooms they'd shared so passionately together without reliving every second in her mind. Spending another evening with him, even though they would be safely chaperoned by two eagle-eyed daughters, was not the way to get her over-active imagination under control.

'All right,' she conceded. 'Provided you promise to get straight down to your homework as soon as we get home.'

She had a feeling that her proviso had been completely lost under the cheers of victory but it was too late now. The two of them were already grabbing their bags and coats and talking at the tops of their voices.

Before she could even open her mouth to remind them to put their coats on Nick was reaching out to first one and then the other to enable them to slide their arms into the sleeves. She gave a silent snort when she saw the docile way they complied, knowing that their response to her own reminder would have been a long-suffering 'Oh, Mum!' and the assertion that they didn't *need* to wear it.

An argument about who would travel with Nick was completely averted when he cheerfully announced that, with Frankie's permission, they were both welcome to climb in.

She was still shaking her head over their fervent pleas when she drew up in the drive beside the house.

What was it about the man that he seemed to be able to wrap everyone around his finger? And it seemed so effortless, too—a part of who he was, rather than what he did.

It had certainly worked on her, more potently than she would ever have believed possible, and now she had the prospect of at least an hour in his company, thanks to her daughters.

Not that it was all bad, she mused when, instead of dumping their belongings on the first available surface, they carefully hung their coats beside his and lined up their wet shoes side by side on the mat.

She was sure she could be permitted a touch of motherly exasperation to see that he had achieved this compliance without saying a word, where all her lectures hadn't worked.

Ah, well. She shrugged as the kettle boiled. New brooms... Familiarity would soon breed contempt and they would be back to their usual untidy ways.

Suddenly she realised where her train of thought had led her and she brought it to a grinding halt.

Familiarity? How would her daughters ever become that familiar with the man? He would soon be married to Vicky Lawrence and any future meetings between them would more than likely be at social events that involved the practice or the hospital. He certainly wouldn't be joining them for family meals without the company of his new wife.

'Anything I can do to help?' he offered from his position propped against the edge of the sink, and she wondered just how long she'd been standing there with all her thoughts running rampant across her face. She hadn't even realised that he'd stayed in the kitchen when Laura and Katie had left.

Before she could formulate an answer there was a coaxing call from the other room.

'Ni-i-ck. Could you help me with my homework? It's science and Mum's *hopeless*!'

'Hopeless at science?' he said with a raised eyebrow, just for Frankie's ears. 'Is that your way of making her do her own work?'

'No. I'm genuinely hopeless,' she admitted as she reached for two mugs and two glasses for juice then turned to open the fridge.

'But…you're a doctor,' he said disbelievingly. 'You had to pass exams in sciences even to start your training.'

'Don't remind me,' she groaned. 'And I hated every minute.'

'So why did you do it? Did your parents push you into training?'

'Not a bit of it,' she retorted, then smiled wryly. 'They thought I was mad to even think about it.'

'So?' he prompted, clearly wanting to know more.

'So, it was the only thing I'd ever wanted to do. So, if it meant that I had to pass sciences…'

'You worked at it until you passed sciences,' he finished for her in a voice grown warm with approval.

'But only after I'd had a long talk with my old family GP,' she explained, uncomfortable with the answering warmth that had wrapped itself around her. 'He confirmed my arrogant adolescent belief that the best GPs aren't necessarily the ones who score the highest academic grades. That they have to have more than their share of empathy and intuition if they're really going to be able to help their patients.'

'And?'

He seemed to be enjoying himself, dragging all this ancient history out of her. She couldn't remember that Martin had ever been in the least bit interested in what had prompted her choice of career or how she had got there.

'And then, as soon as I'd passed my exams, I promptly resolved that I was never going to learn another scientific formula ever again.'

'Not even to help your daughters with their homework?' he taunted, straightening away from his comfortable slouch as she held out a steaming mug.

He wrapped both hands around it and flicked a silent glance at her. He'd made no comment about the fact that she'd remembered just how he liked his coffee but the significance was there in the intensity of his blue eyes.

'Not even to help my daughters,' she said while she tried to ignore those eyes. 'I would never be sure that I was telling them the right thing and it would only muddle them. Far better that they go back to their teacher to get it right.'

'Ni-i-ck?' Laura called again in tones of despair.

'Any objections to me going to see what she's stuck on? I can't guarantee that I'd be any help.'

'Feel free. Oh, and if you could take these through

to them at the same time.' She put the glasses of juice on a small tray and quickly added some cored quarters of apple.

The kitchen seemed much larger once he'd left but suddenly it also seemed lonelier, and she couldn't stop herself from standing a little closer to the door to listen for his voice.

Remembering Martin's impatience with the children when he came home from work wasn't really fair. They had been so much younger then and more demanding.

Still, she couldn't help admiring the way Nick persuaded Laura to explain her problem to him so that *she* was the one who worked the answer out. The fact that he did that in spite of Katie's frequent interruptions was nothing short of miraculous. She knew exactly how difficult it could be, even for someone who was accustomed to their ways.

Suddenly, she found herself standing in front of the sink with her hands clenched so tightly that her knuckles showed white through the skin.

'Don't!' she whispered harshly, the sound of the word startling her almost as much as the sight of the raw pain in her reflection in the window-pane.

Don't be too perfect, she begged, careful to keep the thought silent this time. *If you fit into my little family too perfectly, I'll never be able to deal with you when you're married. I'll always be thinking about might-have-beens.*

Memories of their evening together were still lingering long after the snow had gone.

It had been a meal unlike any other, full of banter and discussion that somehow managed to involve all of them despite the range of ages and interests.

After the meal, Nick had automatically started to clear the table, which in turn had prompted the girls to lend a hand without a word being spoken.

Frankie had thought the politically correct fairy story had been the ideal, if rather hilarious finale, but it had been the last few minutes before Nick had left that had lingered longest and sweetest in her memory.

'I understand now,' he'd said softly, pausing suddenly in the middle of donning his thick jacket to face her.

He'd taken the solitary step that had brought him close enough to cup her cheek in one warm hand and had stood gazing down at her for several timeless seconds.

The gentle contact had left Frankie speechless, but it hadn't mattered. He'd seemed to need the time to put his thoughts in order.

'I've never spent any time with children—at least, not this age or this healthy.' He grinned suddenly, obviously remembering the hilarity they'd shared over his silly story. 'I hadn't realised what miracles they are, Frankie. Real little people complete with their own personalities and opinions, ready to take on the world, and it's all down to the way you're raising them.'

Embarrassment had Frankie shaking her head but he tightened his hold.

'Yes, it is,' he contradicted. 'I can see so much of you in them, and I can fully understand why you were so...' He paused sharply, then continued on a slightly different track. 'I can see now why the thought of losing custody was like having your heart torn out of your chest.'

She had the strange feeling that there was something

he wasn't saying, something more than empathy that had put a shadow in his eyes.

'I'm going to fight him,' she announced, stepping back so that she broke the contact between the two of them, his words of praise injecting a renewed surge of determination. 'He might think he's got all the cards stacked in his favour, but I've been caring for them since before they were born, and I'm not going to meekly hand them over now.'

'Meekly?' he repeated teasingly as he turned towards the door. 'I don't think you know the word. I'm looking forward to hearing that you've won. In the meantime, if you ever need someone to sit with those two, I'd be very upset if I wasn't given first refusal. They're great.'

'So, Nick, when's the wedding? Have you and Vicky set a date yet?' Norman Castle was demanding as Frankie pushed the door open.

As usual, she was juggling with far too many bags, and would have liked to have blamed that for dropping the one containing her lunch with a resounding thud. She could also try to blame the fact that it was Friday, again, and she was due to spend yet another weekend without Laura and Katie.

Unfortunately, she knew that neither excuse would be true. The *real* reason why she'd dropped her bag had been the sudden clench of emotion that had started happening each time she heard someone mention Nick's and Vicky's wedding.

The trouble was, it was happening with monotonous regularity these days. Almost every time she came into the staffroom it seemed to be the favourite topic of conversation…hardly surprising given the interest everyone took in each other's lives around here.

So why was she letting it get to her? Why was she taking it so personally?

It wasn't as if there was anything between herself and Nick—well, apart from the memories that she was determined to wipe from her mind. Unfortunately, she was discovering that it was one thing to spend her days stifling the images as soon as they tried to surface, but another thing entirely to stop them taking over her dreams.

Over the last two weeks she'd started dreading waking up in the morning. It wasn't just that she was exhausted with tossing and turning all night, but that she always seemed to wake too soon and resented finding out that there was no warm, willing man making the blood sing in her veins.

And she felt so guilty all the time.

It was bad enough that she was having such X-rated dreams, but the fact that she was dreaming about another woman's fiancé just didn't sit well with her.

And there he was, sprawled bonelessly in one of the disreputable, squashy, old armchairs that Norman had insisted on rescuing from the old GP practice, apparently completely unaffected by regrets or illicit desires.

If she hadn't been attracted to the man she could almost have disliked him.

'You'll have to ask Vicky about that,' he told Norman, giving the same answer she'd heard several times now. 'Perhaps she'll tell you so you can let me know,' he added, much to Frankie's surprise. It was an even bigger surprise to her that she actually felt a strange sense of relief that the two of them hadn't yet set a date. As if it was any of her business.

Norman laughed. 'Giving you a taste of your own medicine, is she? You kept her waiting all those years before you proposed, now she's keeping you waiting for the wedding.'

'Perhaps that's what it is,' he agreed with a smile of his own, but even from the other side of the room Frankie couldn't help noticing the shadows in his eyes.

She could hardly claim to know the man, but over the last couple of weeks she had recognised that he was an honourable person and she knew that he must be feeling just as guilty and as unhappy with the situation as she was.

Suddenly, she understood that ignoring what had happened might *not* be the best way to deal with it after all. She certainly hadn't been able to put it out of her mind, and was only now realising that they did need to talk.

Of course, as soon as she'd made the decision, it seemed as if everything was conspiring against her as she tried to find a moment to speak to Nick without an audience.

If it wasn't another member of staff lingering for a chat, it was a patient arriving early, or another needing to speak to him about worrying side-effects to a change in medication.

The strange thing was, she had the feeling that he was just as frustrated by events as she was, almost as if they'd come to the same decision at the same time.

By the time she'd spent an hour wandering aimlessly around her house in the wake of Laura's and Katie's departure, she was ready to scream. Unless she found some way of 'accidentally' bumping into him, she wasn't going to see him for at least two days. Anyway, even if she did see him around Edenthwaite, he would have Vicky with him, and she could hardly bring up the topic of his unfaithfulness in front of his fiancée.

'I shall pamper myself,' she announced to the empty room with a flash of inspiration and, after a quick detour by way of the fridge, set off up the stairs.

'I shall have a deep bath full of bubbles and surround myself with candlelight and I shall lie there for hours with some soothing music playing and a glass of wine in my hand.'

Of course, the last part depended on whether the half-bottle of cheap plonk she'd retrieved from the back of the fridge was still drinkable. She couldn't remember when she'd opened it so had no idea exactly how long it had been there. It wasn't as if relaxing glasses of wine were exactly the norm for a working mother of two nearly-teenagers.

Just for tonight, she was going to avoid thinking about how many lonely evenings there would be if Martin succeeded in his plans. Tonight, she was going to revel in the luxury of a quiet house and unlimited time in the bathroom without having to mediate between the two very different emerging characters of her daughters as they fought for dominance.

Except, it didn't work out that way.

Oh, the bath was deep and hot and the bubbles were fragrant and plentiful and the wine was actually drinkable. Unfortunately, the music she'd chosen was a favourite CD of blues played on alto and tenor saxophone and the haunting melodies only seemed to intensify her feelings of loneliness.

It only took five minutes for her to feel depressed and at the end of ten she was close to tears as she contemplated the way her life seemed to have fallen apart over the last few weeks.

It was almost a relief to hear the sound of the door-
bell echoing up the stairs.

She narrowly avoided sending a tidal wave of froth
over the edge of the bath as she leapt out and her hasty
attempt at drying herself was so makeshift that it was
almost impossible to push her arms in the sleeves of
the waiting dressing gown.

That had been another mistake. It wasn't her usual
ratty towelling one, but the sumptuous black silk with
the gold embroidery that she'd lent to Nick that fateful
afternoon.

She'd told herself that it was crazy not to put it to
good use, but all she had to do was look at the wretched
thing and she could see Nick wearing it. Now she was
wrapping it around herself as she scurried out of the
candlelit bathroom into the relative darkness of the
landing, and trying to tie the slippery sash to hold it in
position without tripping over the ends.

She completely forgot what she was supposed to be
doing when she caught sight of her visitor through the
window at the top of the stairs. Its position gave her a
perfect view of the well-lit driveway and the lean, long-
legged man walking away from her house.

Before she thought what she was doing she'd
reached out to rap on the window, suddenly desperate
to attract his attention before he could climb into his
car and leave.

It worked.

Her hand was still hovering in mid-air when he
turned, and as if he knew exactly where she would be,
his eyes seemed to find her without a moment's hesitation.

For several seconds they stood there, Frankie at the
window with her hair all damp around the back of her

neck where the bubbles had wet it, and Nick in the driveway with his dark hair ruffled by the spiteful wind that seemed to have been blowing from the Arctic all day.

As if they had come to a decision, they both began to move, Nick returning towards the house while Frankie's feet had her flying down the stairs without a thought for safety.

They met by the back door, Nick standing with his hands on his hips when she pulled the door open, the soft buttery light from the alcove by the cooker painting each lean plane of his face with a loving touch.

She had little time to notice that the bitter chocolate colour of his leather jacket almost perfectly matched his hair, or that his blue shirt was only one shade lighter than his eyes.

'Frankie?' he murmured as those eyes skimmed over her from head to foot then began the return journey at a far more leisurely pace, apparently oblivious of the bitter cold swirling around them.

By the time he reached her face his gaze was dark with his awareness of where she had been and what she had been doing when he'd rung the bell, and she was shaking deep inside with her reaction to the heated intensity.

When he took a pace towards her she was helpless to do anything other than step aside to allow him to enter her home, her sanctuary, knowing instinctively that she was offering far more.

'Frankie,' he said again, but this time the word was a growl as he scooped her off her feet and into his arms.

If he hadn't swung the door shut behind him she wouldn't have remembered. All she could think about was that he was here and she was in his arms when she'd never thought it would happen again.

'Nick,' she whimpered as she reached up to wrap her arms around his neck, her head already angled to receive his kiss.

For just a second, as his lips met hers, it felt like coming home, but then the heat of overwhelming desire struck them like a detonation. Suddenly, a kiss was never going to be enough and they were both fighting to get closer, desperate to get rid of anything that would prevent them touching, stroking, possessing, becoming one.

Her dressing-gown was easily disposed of. She'd been in too much of a hurry to come down the stairs to him to manage to tie the sash properly, and a single tug left her completely exposed to his ravening hands.

She tried to fathom the intricacies of shirt buttons but when that was too slow she just grabbed two handfuls of fabric and dragged it up out of his waistband to reveal the taut muscles of his chest to her hands and eyes.

Soon, her desperation to touch, to stroke, to explore couldn't be satisfied with limited access to his chest alone but her hands were trembling too much to allow more than fumbling attempts to unfasten his belt.

'Here,' he growled as his hand replaced hers, the sound of his zip the most welcome punctuation to their hurried breathing and impatient moans.

Frankie was desperate to feel his body against hers, his raw masculine warmth pressed tightly against the perfumed softness of hers. Then he bent to lift her and she eagerly wrapped her arms tightly around him again as he turned so that her back was braced against the wall.

'Hold tight,' he instructed, his edgy tone telling her more than words how tightly his nerves were strung as he guided her legs around his hips.

For just a fraction of a second she marvelled at what they were doing, unable to believe that they were about to make love just inches from her back door. Then he was joining their bodies together and all she could think about was how utterly right it felt to have him inside her again, as though she had been made for just this man and had been waiting all these years to find him.

The pace was far too frantic to last and all too soon she was hearing the echoes of her own cry of satisfaction blending with his.

'Damn,' he muttered into the side of her neck, his chest rising and falling against hers as he fought for breath. 'I didn't mean to do that.'

At the sound of his regret, Frankie went rigid in his grasp and turned her head away as she felt the searing heat of embarrassment sweep over her.

That was the last thing she'd expected him to say. Surely she hadn't been the only one to experience that cataclysmic explosion.

'Frankie?'

She couldn't answer. There weren't any words, but with their bodies still intimately joined there was no way she could avoid the hand that insisted she turn her head to face him.

'Did I hurt you?' he demanded fiercely, his eyes burning into her like blue flames. 'Damn, Frankie, I'm sorry. I know it shouldn't have happened and I'm going to feel as guilty as hell later, but I just couldn't stop.'

He shook his head and would have stepped back to

release her but something in his face made her tighten her grip with the last of her strength.

'You couldn't stop?' she said weakly. Sudden warmth began to spread through her but she needed to be sure.

'What do you think, woman?' he demanded roughly, casting a telling glance down at the way their bodies were plastered so tightly together. 'You can't come to the door wearing nothing more than black silk and expect me to keep my hands to myself.'

'So you're not sorry that it happened?' she asked, cringing at the uncertainty she could still hear in her own voice. Wasn't it bad enough that Martin had left her in no doubt about her lack of attractiveness to the opposite sex, without letting Nick know that she realised her shortcomings?

'God, no!' he exclaimed with ego-stroking promptness. 'I don't regret *that*... Just that it *happened* like that...'

When she realised that he was genuinely upset, Frankie couldn't stop the smile that crept over her face.

'Did it never enter your head that I might have liked it happening like *that*?' she asked softly, some imp prompting her to tighten herself around him as she spoke. Her smile widened when she felt his response deep inside her. 'Anyway, who says it's all over?' she teased as she flexed her muscles again.

'Witch!' he accused on a surprised chuckle, and Frankie was delighted to feel that he wasn't able to stop his response the second time either. 'Can't you at least let us get somewhere more comfortable before we start again?'

He tightened his arms around her, pulling her even more securely against him before he turned, his eyes scanning the kitchen. He'd only taken a couple of steps in the direction of the sturdy kitchen table where she shared so many meals with Laura and Katie when Frankie realised where he was taking her.

'No, Nick. Not there,' she said hastily. 'I'd never be able to look my daughters in the face again.'

He closed his eyes and groaned, pressing his forehead against hers as though he was reaching the end of his tether.

She knew how he felt. They should both have found satisfaction with that explosive mating but all it seemed to have done was whetted their appetite to an even keener edge.

'Nick?' She was overwhelmingly aware of the intimacy of their position and so desperate to do something about it that she was even starting to weaken in her resolve when he opened his eyes.

For just a moment he looked down at her with a wicked glint in his eyes. It was all too obvious that he knew that he could persuade her if he tried, and she knew that he wouldn't have to try very hard.

At the last moment, when the tension between them was growing close to flash point, he relented, whirling to leave the kitchen before they gave in to their common urge to begin the mating dance all over again.

CHAPTER FIVE

THE light shining through from the bathroom wasn't very strong in Frankie's bedroom but it was enough for Nick to be able to watch her as she slept.

What was it about this woman that affected him so strongly?

She was only five feet two inches to his nearly six feet but she packed a punch like TNT that detonated all his hard-fought resolution into oblivion.

He'd come here today knowing that Laura and Katie were due to spend the weekend with their father. What he had to say to Frankie was best discussed without the possibility that they might be interrupted or, even worse, overheard.

So, what had happened to his determination that they'd sit down to talk like sane rational adults?

Frankie had happened, that's what. All he'd needed had been one glimpse of her curvy little body wrapped in gold-embroidered black silk and he hadn't been able to resist, especially when he'd seen in her whisky-coloured eyes that she'd wanted the same thing.

He sent a leisurely glance over the body snuggled so sweetly next to his, knowing that if she were awake she would be reaching for something to cover herself.

He smiled, wondering how long it would take him to convince her that she had absolutely nothing to be ashamed of. She was everything lush and womanly and sexy that any man could desire. His own body's reaction to her proximity was testament to that, in spite of the fact that it should by rights be totally exhausted by now.

The strange thing was, it was the first time that he'd ever been attracted to a woman who wasn't tall, slim, blonde and blue-eyed. Both Vicky and Elinore could have come out of the same mould, as pretty and apparently delicate as Dresden figurines.

It was amazing how deceptive looks could be, he mused with a flash of the sort of wisdom that sometimes arrived in the small hours of the night. Elinore had hidden a core of lies and deception underneath her sweet fragility while Vicky hid a core of pure steely determination.

Frankie was a different kettle of fish altogether with her dark hair cut into short feathery layers and eyes that could flash from the soothing sweetness of honey to the burning bite of whisky in a flash.

Sometimes it was difficult to reconcile the woman uncertain of her own sexual powers with the experienced mother of two soon-to-be teenagers.

Just the thought of Laura and Katie was enough to put a smile on his face. They were great kids and the more he saw of them, the better they seemed to get. Laura had been the more wary at first and he hadn't been sure whether it was because she was the elder or because she was naturally the more cautious of the two.

Perhaps it had something to do with the family history. Maybe she'd been old enough to remember her father's defection and was less trusting as a result.

There was no such problem with Katie. She had taken to him with all the exuberance of a lively puppy right from the first time he'd collected them from school.

Over the last couple of weeks he'd even begun to

volunteer to fetch them when he was free, enjoying their conversations and fascinated by their innocent points of view.

When Laura had opened up enough to ask for his opinion he'd been struck by totally unexpected feelings of nervousness and pride—fear that he didn't know enough about children to be able to give advice and pride that she felt that she could ask.

'If I *can* help, I will,' he'd temporised hastily. 'But wouldn't your mother be able to help?'

'Not really.' She'd grimaced, the expression so like one he'd seen on her mother's face that he'd found it hard not to smile. 'You see, I'm trying to decide what to do when I'm old enough to go to university.'

She'd looked so earnest that he'd known he mustn't laugh, but what on earth was she doing, worrying about this *now*?

'Laura, you're still at junior school. There'll be plenty of time to make those sorts of decisions when you've taken a few exams.'

'I'll be going to senior school later this year,' she pointed out seriously. 'And Dad said I would have to choose my subject options according to what career I wanted to follow.'

Nick was seized with a sudden desire to box the wretched man's ears. He might be the child's father, but he didn't seem to know her well enough to see that she was already such a solemn little thing. She should be enjoying her childhood, not worrying about career choices that were still several years away.

'So, have you had any ideas of what you'd like to do, or is it just a matter of knowing what subjects you enjoy most?' He had a feeling that he knew what it must be like to pick a path across quicksand. Each step or, in his case, each word could lead to disaster.

'I think I'd be good as a lawyer or as a doctor,' she announced earnestly. 'But that's the problem.'

'Why is it a problem? You already know from your parents that they're both excellent careers.'

'That's why,' she said with another grimace. 'If I choose doctor, my dad will be disappointed, and if I choose lawyer, then Mum will. I can't please both of them but I don't want to upset either of them.'

'Then you haven't got a problem at all,' he said firmly. 'When you're choosing your career, there's only one person whose opinion you need to think about, and that's you.'

'Me?' She blinked, clearly startled with the idea.

'Yes, Laura. You,' he repeated with a reassuring smile. 'It's going to be your life, not theirs. So, any decision about what you want to do with it must be one that makes *you* happy. Then you have to make up your mind that, whatever you do, you're going to be the best you can be. If you're a lawyer, be a *good* lawyer; if you're a doctor, be a *good* doctor. Whatever you decide, go into it with your heart and soul. That's why it's so important that it's something *you* want to do.'

Seeing the smile creep over her face was like watching the sun come through after a storm.

'So, that's my opinion. Did it help?' he asked, hoping he hadn't come on too strong and hoping, too, that Frankie wouldn't think he'd been interfering where he wasn't welcome.

'Oh, yes,' she said fervently. 'I hadn't thought of it like that before, but it all makes sense now. It's *my* life, so it's *my* choice.'

Nick wondered if he ought to have added a rider that sometimes expert advice could help make decisions easier but Katie had run out of patience with her big sister monopolising his attention and the moment was lost.

She wasn't one to worry about eventual career choices when there was the prospect of a willing pair of ears to hear her read or listen to the latest episode in the saga of her constantly shifting friendships.

She'd even started a pointed campaign to get him invited home for a meal each time he played chauffeur, and sometimes he wasn't sure whether he was relieved or disappointed that he was rarely free to take her up on it.

After last night perhaps he ought to reorganise his timetable a little to make sure he was available when the invitations came. He was almost certain that Frankie would probably confirm an invitation made by her daughter and he would enjoy the chance to spend more time with all three of them.

He closed his eyes a moment but Frankie's welcome the night before was still there in his mind's eye, all warm silky skin and so heart-stoppingly eager for his kisses and his touch.

What on earth had made him try to persuade himself that one night would be enough? Last night, their second spent together, had only nurtured the suspicion that a lifetime wouldn't be enough.

He sighed, weary more from his weighty thoughts than from the mind-blowing activities of the night.

Was he really such a fickle man?

One moment he was proposing to Vicky, the young woman who had patiently loved him for more years than he liked to think about. They were in the middle of planning their wedding, for heaven's sake…or at least Vicky's mother was, if she could ever get him and the strangely elusive Vicky together long enough to make a few decisions.

Yet here he was, in bed with another woman and admitting that his fascination with her would probably take a lifetime to run its course.

The thought was enough to stop him in his tracks. If he loved Vicky enough to marry her, what was he doing here with Frankie? If he was admitting that his attraction was far more than a mindless one-night stand…and he was proud to be able to say that he'd never indulged in one of those…then what was he doing engaged to Vicky?

He was ashamed to admit that what he was doing wasn't fair to either of them, but honest enough to realise that the situation had been prompted by something far more potent than mere lust.

Not that there was anything wrong with the lusty feelings that swept over him each time he looked at Frankie. They were a normal male reaction to a woman who attracted him, and she certainly attracted him— had done from the first glimpse he'd had of her when she'd been soaking wet, washing the car.

Prompted by the memory, his eyes skimmed over her sleeping form, tracing her slender shoulders and the curve into her waist, the lush fullness of her breasts and the womanly flare of her hips.

He stifled a groan as his body started to react in an all too predictable way but he needn't have bothered. As if she was tuned to his thoughts Frankie started to wake, brushing against him as she stretched her arms unselfconsciously over her head.

He couldn't resist her.

His hand was already cupping her as he leant forward to murmur a greeting against her lips. Without hesitation she opened to him, mouth and body, and he was instantly consumed by the need for more.

She was draped bonelessly over his panting body when he finally remembered the primary reason why he'd turned up on her doorstep in the first place and he groaned aloud.

How could he have forgotten? And not only that, but he'd spent the night compounding the potential problem.

'Exhausted?' she purred in his ear then nibbled the lobe, sending an impossible surge of renewed arousal through him.

'Have mercy, woman,' he pleaded even as he cupped her hips and pressed her closer.

'I thought younger men were supposed to have more stamina?' she teased, squirming provocatively.

'Depends whether you're looking for quality or quantity,' he fired back on a growl, already mentally calculating whether they had enough time to complete what his body would like to start. Heaven only knew how many times they'd made love since that first explosive episode just inside her kitchen door.

With that thought, sanity returned with all the effect of a bucket of icy water, stopping him in his tracks.

'Um, Frankie,' he began, suddenly finding it hard to put words together. It was difficult to admit just how thoughtless he'd been, not once but over and over again. 'You are taking something, aren't you?'

'Taking something?' she repeated idly, her concentration evidently more on the finger that was tracing the whorls of dark hair around one of his nipples.

'The Pill?' he prompted. 'Or did you have a coil

fitted?' They'd been far too intimate for him to have missed the existence of any of the more obvious barrier methods of contraception.

He felt her whole body grow tense and had a sudden sinking feeling deep in his gut.

She lifted her head from the comfortable niche in the angle of his neck and he saw the echoes of pain darkening her eyes.

'I've never needed to take anything,' she said softly, obviously finding it hard to hold his gaze.

'What? Never?' In spite of the seriousness of the situation, he was intrigued.

'Martin was going to take care of things until we were ready to start a family, but I became pregnant on our honeymoon.' An endearing blush spread up over her face at the admission, but he couldn't allow himself to be distracted. This was too important.

'Then, after Katie was born, I didn't get pregnant again even though we didn't take any precautions. I would have liked another baby but…'

Her words died away on a sad little shrug, and he was struck by the unexpected wish that he could have been the one to give her the child she'd wanted.

He had a sudden image of her body swollen and lush with the evidence of the infant growing inside her—a child that he'd fathered—and his heart seemed to leap right up into his throat.

That impossible idea was swiftly submerged under the relief that he hadn't jeopardised her through his thoughtlessness. Neither of them could afford the complications that an accidental pregnancy would entail—not Frankie, with her husband about to fight for a change in their children's custody, nor himself, with his wedding to Vicky in the throes of organisation.

His wedding to Vicky...

Suddenly, as he looked into the face of the woman in his arms, he knew with a soul-deep certainty that the wedding couldn't go ahead, at least not in the near future.

Since meeting Frankie, he'd been doing a lot of thinking. Admittedly, his hormones were playing a part, but logic was also telling him that there was something missing in his relationship with Vicky.

For heaven's sake, he'd known her for years and they'd been engaged for months but he'd never felt so desperate to make love with her that he couldn't get further than the back door. For all Jack's sly comments, Nick hadn't so much as hinted that he and Vicky hadn't done much more than kiss. In fact, now that he thought about it, he wouldn't be at all surprised if their wedding night revealed the fact that she was still a virgin.

Not that it was his lack of opportunities that had drawn him to Frankie. He liked to think that he'd never allowed his hormones to do his thinking for him, but...there was something about this woman that called to him on a soul-deep level that he was powerless to fight.

'As for sexually transmitted diseases...' she said, continuing as though there hadn't been a break in their conversation. Perhaps there hadn't. He had no idea how long it had taken for that tangle of thoughts to unravel in his mind. 'You don't have to worry about that either, because the only other man I've ever slept with was Martin, and the last time was long before he left me over seven years ago.'

Nick had sensed that she wasn't very experienced and had probably realised on a subconscious level that a working mother with two young children wouldn't have had much time for an active sex life. What he hadn't been prepared for was the sudden wave of possessiveness that swept over him.

He might only be the second man to have made love with her but he found himself fighting a crazy wish that he'd been the *only* man in her life.

What on earth was going on here? Was it just euphoria after a night of magic? If so, why hadn't it ever happened before?

'Apart from my youth when, like most young men, I made impossible boasts about my prowess, I've only been involved twice, the last time more than a year and a half ago,' he admitted candidly. Unexpectedly, he felt the need to tell her something that would let her know what sort of man he was on the inside. 'In each case, I thought the relationship would lead to something more…permanent.'

'Marriage?' she prompted softly, her face and voice so expressionless that he was almost certain that she was controlling them deliberately.

The thought that Frankie might not be so calm about the idea of him being involved with other women was a definite boost to his ego.

'I hoped so, at the time,' he said dismissively, then stayed silent, wondering whether she would be able to resist the urge to pursue it.

'So…what happened?' It had taken several seconds for her to succumb and he had to hide a small smile of triumph.

'The first time we were just too young—barely out of our teens and with far too much study still left in front of us. I think we ended up spending more time in the laundrette than we did with each other.'

'And the second?'

The memory of what Elinore had nearly done to his career was still sharp enough to make him wince.

'We discovered that we had different goals, different ambitions and we couldn't agree on…on what we were willing to sacrifice to achieve them.'

The words were deliberately ambiguous but even so he was surprised to hear himself say them. He hadn't even contemplated telling Vicky the extent of Elinore's perfidy and when he realised that he was seriously tempted to tell Frankie the whole story he knew it was time to pull back.

Too fast, too intense, his mind was telling him, even as something deep inside was urging him to race ahead to see where this new path in his life was leading.

The sudden intrusion of a high-pitched bleeping broke his train of thought, and the strangely companionable way they had been lying so close to each other was destroyed when Frankie had to turn away to silence the alarm.

'You're on duty this morning?' he asked, disappointed at the end of their time together.

'Not today. That's the time I have to get up every day if the girls and I are going to get everything done.'

'I suppose, with only one bathroom and three females needing to get ready,' he teased, just to see her whisky-coloured eyes flash fire. Then he grinned as he added, 'It might save time if we shared.'

Frankie made a scoffing sound as she stretched out one arm to try to reach the softly gleaming pile of black silk fabric just out of her reach.

Nick couldn't help smiling. The two of them had been as intimate as it was possible for a man and woman to be and she was still concerned about walking to the bathroom without a gown to cover her nudity. It was just one more endearing facet to the complex person called Frankie.

'Here. Let me,' he offered, deliberately remaining naked as he walked around the end of the bed to hand the dressing-gown to her.

He could have predicted the way her eyes would initially widen when she caught sight of him, and then would swiftly be turned away while a wash of soft colour highlighted her cheeks. He also knew that within seconds she wouldn't be able to resist looking at him again, and that her eyes would darken with growing desire the longer she looked.

'Join me?' he offered, holding out his hand and waiting to see what she would do.

He couldn't help groaning aloud when she flipped back the covers and allowed him to pull her to her feet as naked as the day she was born.

'Woman, you're going to kill me,' he growled as he swooped to lift her into his arms and set off for the bathroom.

By the time they were both standing under the pelting spray with exploring hands completely forgetting about the use of soap, he suddenly realised that he felt more alive than he ever had in his life.

Frankie knew that what she and Nick were doing was wrong and that she shouldn't be allowing it to happen, but at some time during the night she had come to a decision.

Nick was a colleague and an engaged man, she reminded herself as she put two slices of bread in the toaster. So it would be totally wrong for the two of them to let two isolated nights turn into any sort of affair and totally unfair to Vicky,

From now on, she thought firmly, she would make sure that they weren't alone together, that they didn't have the opportunity for any sexual intimacy.

Except, for the first time in her life she wanted to be totally selfish.

For years she'd been the responsible GP, wife and mother who barely took the time to have her hair cut, never mind pamper herself.

Nick was something totally unprecedented, like a bright star exploding into the darkness of her life, and she was so tempted to bask in his glow while she could.

But it was wrong. Already, she'd found that she couldn't catch sight of Vicky without feeling the flush of guilt heating her cheeks, and with every little detail about the impending wedding discussed at great length, she could hardly ignore the fact that Nick belonged to someone else.

'Frankie?'

His deep voice drew her out of her uncomfortable thoughts to find that she'd managed to set the table and present a picture-perfect breakfast without remembering doing any of it.

He was standing barefoot just inside the doorway with one shoulder propped against the wall, his folded arms giving an impression of ease completely at odds with the intent expression in his dark blue eyes. In the absence of any clean clothes he'd had to don the slightly crumpled shirt he'd discarded so cavalierly last night, and with his damp hair beginning to dry into a series of unruly waves he looked totally devastating.

'Nick. Come and sit down,' she invited, quickly turning away from the tempting sight as though there was some job left to do.

She hoped he couldn't hear the bitter-sweet emotions

churning inside her when she realised that this would
be the last time this could happen. It might feel right
to have him here like this, but he didn't belong. His
life lay in another direction, with another woman.

Vicky. Her colleague at Denison Memorial. Pretty,
bright, loving Vicky who had loved Nick for so many
years and was finally going to marry him.

'Oh, this is perfect,' Nick groaned as he tucked into
his food. 'If you only knew how long it is since I had
an English breakfast like this.'

'I don't do it very often because of the cholesterol
thing, but sometimes I give myself a treat when the
girls are away and I'm not on duty.'

'Well, my taste buds thank you,' he said with another moan of appreciation. 'I've even tried ordering it
in restaurants but nothing tastes like a genuine home-
cooked English breakfast.'

Somehow, seeing him enjoying her cooking so
openly seemed to untie some of the knots inside her
and she was actually able to sit down to start her own
meal. As long as she didn't allow herself to think about
all the mornings when he was going to be sitting down
to eat with Vicky…

No, not until there was nothing left but the toast
crumbs was she going to allow the outside world to
intrude. This was going to be a last little oasis of time
that they spent together and she was going to hoard
every second of it like a miser so that she could take
it out in her memory and savour it in the years to come.

'Frankie?'

Something in Nick's voice suddenly sent a shiver up
the back of her neck, snapping her out of her fanciful
thoughts in an instant.

'I've been doing a lot of thinking,' he continued, his

eyes focused far too intently on the tip of his finger as he pushed the pale golden crumbs into a pile.

So have I, she thought sadly, her heart growing heavy as she realised that he was actually going to put those thoughts into words.

She should have expected it, really.

In spite of their crazy reaction to each other, she knew that he was really a very honourable man. He wouldn't dream of walking out after the hours they'd just spent together without saying something.

'I'm not quite sure where to start,' he admitted with a soft laugh that almost sounded like disbelief. He shook his head then looked up from his preoccupation with the crumbs to fix her with a determined gaze. 'First, you have to know that nothing like this has ever happened to me before.'

'Not even when you were young and foolish?' she challenged, but her heart wasn't in it. At least he was offering a sop to her vanity, that she'd been something out of the ordinary in his life.

'*Especially* not when I was young and foolish,' he retorted seriously, before adding with a wicked grin, 'I wouldn't have seen further than the fact that it was the best sex I've ever had in my life.'

Me, too, she thought with feeling, but one part of her wished she'd never experienced it because now she would know what she was missing.

'But it's not *just* that,' he continued, reaching out to capture her hand.

The warm strength in those long fingers and the tender way they cradled her own much smaller hand was just another scene to store away for the barren future.

'There's something…something special between us.

Something that makes me feel as if I've known you for years, rather than just two weeks. I've known Vicky since she was fourteen, but…' Nick shook his head, a frown pleating his forehead.

As soon as he mentioned his fiancée it felt as if a giant hand clenched around Frankie's heart. It was enough to know that he was going to marry the woman without having to listen to a litany of her good points and the tale of how their love had grown over the years.

'Anyway,' he continued, tightening his hand around hers, 'I've decided that the only thing to do is call off the engagement.'

'What?' Frankie sat up with a jerk, unable to believe what she'd just heard.

'I said, I'm going to speak to Vicky to tell her—'

'No, Nick! You can't!' she exclaimed frantically as renewed guilt flooded through her. She snatched her hand back out of his grasp, unable to bear the sweet torment of the contact any longer.

'Nick, just because you and I…because we…gave in to temptation…' Oh, why was it so difficult to find the words she wanted when she wanted them? 'That doesn't mean you have to break her heart. She's been waiting for you for twelve years. *Twelve years!* If neither of us says anything and…and if we make certain to keep away from each other, there's no reason why this…this whatever-it-is between us won't die a natural death.'

He was silent for so long that she was ready to scream, those dark blue eyes gazing at her face so intently that she grew uncomfortable.

Could he tell that one small corner of her treacherous heart was actually singing at the thought that he was willing to break his engagement?

'I don't know if we can put that sort of distance between us,' he pointed out finally. 'We have to work together, part of the team at Denison Memorial. What are people going to think if they see one of us scurrying out of a room as soon as the other appears? And you can bet it wouldn't take long before someone noticed.'

Frankie pulled a face, knowing he was right. It *was* going to be difficult, especially when she wanted nothing more than to spend her time with him.

'Anyway,' he continued doggedly, 'I don't want to cut myself off from you because that would also inevitably mean cutting myself off from Laura and Katie. And who says I want this…"*whatever-it-is*" between us to die a natural death? Perhaps I want to see if it can survive and grow.'

'Nick, no!' She covered her face with her hands. 'I'm pleased that you want to see the girls—they like you, too. But this isn't about you and me. You can't let a couple of…of one-night stands knock your life off course. I won't let you.'

As she watched, it almost seemed as if a shutter came down somewhere behind his eyes, and for the first time since she'd turned round with the hose in her hand, she had absolutely no idea what he was thinking. It wasn't until there wasn't even a hint of a smile lurking there that she realised just how often she was accustomed to seeing one.

'Is that what those nights were to you?' he demanded softly, the icy edge to his voice sending a shiver up her spine. 'Can you really dismiss them as nothing more than a meaningless roll in the hay?'

'I *have* to,' she retorted, humiliated to feel scalding tears flooding her eyes. 'Don't you see?'

'No. I don't,' he snapped, raking one exasperated

hand through his hair to leave it standing up in every direction. 'So perhaps you'd better explain it to me.'

'Nick, please... I'm a divorced mother of two who's facing the prospect of having her children taken away, and you're already on your way to the altar with the woman you've known for twelve years.'

She had to pause while she fought for control, fought to make him understand. 'It doesn't matter how much I enjoyed our time together. It doesn't matter that I've never known anything like it and probably never will again. What matters is that I've got to find some way of parcelling this...this *episode* in my life out of sight before it causes a disaster. Otherwise, I'd never be able to live with the guilt.'

CHAPTER SIX

FRANKIE felt almost guilty when the practice was suddenly inundated with a flu epidemic.

She'd been praying for some way to keep away from Nick, and this proved to be the ideal excuse. None of the members in the practice had enough time to breathe, let alone spend time arguing over the inarguable.

'At least the epidemic waited until the snow was gone,' Jack Lawrence grumbled as he stumbled into the staff lounge, then groaned as he lowered himself into a chair. 'Either I'm getting old or lack of sleep is finally catching up with me.'

'It comes to us all—the day when you realise that you'd rather go home to sleep alone, just to recharge your batteries,' Frankie teased, then turned serious. After all, he might be a bit of a playboy but he was a colleague and she genuinely liked him. 'Jack, are you sure you're not coming down with the flu yourself?'

'Nothing so simple,' he groaned. 'It's just that I ache all over and I haven't had any fun getting like this.'

She knew how he felt.

The last week had been a killer, especially as some of their patients lived out in the wilds of the Cumbrian countryside. A home visit to check on someone exhibiting the early signs of pleurisy or pneumonia might not take very long, but the length of time it took to get to an isolated farmhouse and then return to the surgery could add an hour or more.

She was beginning to feel as if she'd done several rounds with a heavyweight boxer, too. *And* she was on call tonight.

The weary silence was suddenly broken by the annoying sound of one of the practice mobile phones. They both groaned as they reached for pockets and handbag but it was Frankie's that had lit up.

The result of the call made her groan even more.

'Trouble?' Jack enquired when she ended the call.

'Big trouble,' she agreed, rubbing her forehead to try to massage away the headache that had been threatening all day. 'I'm on call tonight and that was my babysitter, telling me she's gone down with this wretched bug.'

'Bad luck. Have you got a back-up sitter?'

For just a second Frankie's subconscious escaped her rigid control and threw Nick's face into focus, but she ruthlessly subdued it again. She'd barely seen him since their last conversation, so he must be spending his time with Vicky. He wouldn't want to keep an eye on Laura and Katie.

'What, you mean other than dragging them around the countryside with me all night?' she said wryly, then sank wearily onto the arm of the nearest chair. 'Maybe I've just been lucky so far but I haven't had a problem before. Since the practice is part of a group covering scheme I'm not on call too often and this is the first time that my sitter has had to call off.'

She ran frustrated hands through her hair, pausing a moment to massage the growing ache at her temples.

'This is the sort of situation that local people don't usually have to face,' she grumbled. 'If they've got family living all around them they can call on any number of people in an emergency. As a single mum, I'm reliant on finding willing employees or my whole system collapses.'

Jack was silent for a moment, just long enough for Frankie to regret sounding off like that. As a single man he didn't really want to know about the arrangements she had to make to enable her to fulfil her duties.

'How big is your couch?' he demanded suddenly, startling her out of her preoccupation.

'My couch?' she repeated stupidly, wondering if a headache could affect her hearing. She must have missed part of the conversation.

'Is it long enough for me to stretch out full length?' he continued. 'Because if it is, and if you can guarantee that your two sleep right through the night and don't need taking to the bathroom, I can just as easily catch up on my rest at your place as mine.'

Frankie blinked, completely taken aback by the unexpected offer. It seemed so out of character for a man who prided himself on being footloose and fancy-free, but it would certainly solve her problem.

'That's very generous of you, but… Are you sure, Jack? If you're so tired, wouldn't you rather be at home in your own bed?'

'What makes you think I can't sleep in any bed?' he teased with a sudden flash of his bad-boy grin. Then he was serious again. 'It's not so long since my medical training that I can't remember how to sleep standing up if I have to. Anyway, Frankie, look on the bright side. There's no telling if you'll even be called out tonight, so we might both get a full night's sleep.'

Frankie was desperate enough not to want to put him off, and with the minimum of fuss they arranged that he would go home to collect an overnight bag and then join her little family for supper.

*　　*　　*

Their peaceful night never happened.

Almost as soon as the practice closed Frankie's mobile phone began to ring with messages from the after-hours service to visit one patient after another.

There was an angina patient whose severe attack wasn't responding to treatment. When she reached his isolated cottage she quickly realised that he needed immediate admission to hospital.

Then it was back to the outskirts of Edenthwaite where there was a young woman barely at the end of the first trimester of her pregnancy with unexpected pain and bleeding. She was in such a state of panic that hospital admission for observation would be the only way to calm her and her frantic husband down.

There was no point trying to explain to the two of them that, wherever she was, bed rest was all that could be offered. Frankie realised that they needed the emotional support of high-tech hospital surroundings while nature took its course. All she could do was hope that things turned out to have a happy ending.

Of course, there were far more calls than necessary from people who thought a home visit and a prescription for antibiotics would magically stop the onset of flu. She was becoming heartily sick of having to explain over and over again that antibiotics weren't the answer, and could actually make the problem worse.

In between, she'd barely had time to stick her head round her front door to check that Laura and Katie had remembered to do their homework and that Jack was coping with the two of them before she was off again. This time the patient was an elderly man with all the painful symptoms of a blocked catheter.

An hysterical mother of a six-month-old with an attack of croup was almost the most draining case, and by the time she left the steam-filled bathroom to a much-relieved mother and child, her clothes were damp right through and she was absolutely limp with exhaustion.

It was almost midnight before Frankie was able to call back at the house again.

She didn't have much hope that she would be able to stay long, not the way her luck was running tonight. At least she would be able to check up to see if Jack was still coping all right, although the fact that he hadn't phoned her must be a good indication that nothing disastrous had happened while he'd been in charge.

When she saw that all the rooms seemed to be in darkness she breathed a sigh of relief. At least her amateur child-minder was catching up on his sleep, she thought as she reversed quietly into the drive to be ready for a quick getaway.

Mindful that she didn't want to wake anyone, she opened the front door as silently as possible, toeing off her shoes just inside the door before she started to creep towards the kitchen.

The fact that the little light had been left on over the cooker didn't worry her. She'd been known to forget it herself. All she was concentrating on was making her way to the kettle when a voice emerged from the darkness beside her, nearly scaring her out of her wits.

'The kettle's just boiled. Tea or coffee?'

'Nick?' she gasped and whirled around, her heart beating so fast it almost felt as if it was going to leap out of her throat.

The light was only just strong enough to reach him, painting sculptural highlights down one side of his clever face and revealing the lean fingers wrapped around a mug on the table.

'Wh-what on earth are you doing here?'

'Jack had to leave,' he said succinctly, and reached out to raise the teapot in her direction. 'Want to get a cup for some of this?'

'Had to leave?' she parroted, automatically turning and reaching into the cupboard for one of her favourite bone china mugs. 'Why? And what are *you* doing here?'

As if he'd been doing it for years, Nick took the mug from her when she offered it and poured the tea exactly the way she liked it.

'He was called in for an obstetric case that turned a bit tricky so he called me to take over here.'

She leant back against the row of cupboards, the edge of the work surface pressing uncomfortably into her back. She ached to sink into a chair to rest her weary body, but even taking a seat on the opposite side of the table would take her far too close to him.

'But why *you*?' she persisted, then suddenly realised she was beginning to sound like a record stuck in the same groove.

'Because he knows that the girls are comfortable with me and wouldn't be frightened if they woke to find me here, so he phoned to find out if I was available,' he said simply.

Just like that, the prosaic reason for his presence became obvious.

For a moment her imagination had been whirling with all sorts of crazy ideas, half of them probably fuelled by their mutual guilt.

Initially, her heart had leapt with fright when his voice had emerged out of the darkness, but it had pounded even harder when she'd realised just who it was sitting in the silent gloom of her kitchen.

For just a moment she'd had to admit to herself that she'd been missing him and had hoped that his presence in her home had meant that he'd been missing her just as much.

Those were the thoughts that needed to be squashed most fiercely.

He was an engaged man with his whole life planned out ahead of him, a life that didn't include her, so she wasn't going to allow herself to miss him any more.

She buried her nose in the warm steam rising from the mug for a moment then forced herself to start some sort of conversation. She might be aware of everything about him, from the rumpled hair and open neck of his shirt to the casual jeans and naked feet splayed under her table, but she would behave as if they were no more than friendly colleagues if it killed her.

'Have you been here long?' she began politely, and could have groaned when she realised how inane it sounded. This wasn't some social wine-and-cheese party, this was the middle of the night in her kitchen with the man who could set her blood on fire with little more than a glance from his deep blue eyes.

'An hour or so. Maybe two,' he replied, equally politely, but she was sure she could see the glint of humour in those eyes.

Tongue-tied and totally unable to think of anything else to say, she felt the silence in the dimly lit room begin to stretch to uncomfortable lengths. Even though she knew that any conversation between them could turn into a minefield, she was almost relieved when he finally spoke.

'Look, Frankie, if there's a bit of a lull in the calls,

do you think it would be a good idea if we went to bed?'

She choked on her tea, gasping and wheezing as a mouthful went down the wrong way.

It didn't help when he leapt to his feet to relieve her of the mug then wrapped a supporting arm around her shoulders.

The temptation to lean against his strength was almost overwhelming but she forced herself to turn away and brace her hands on the edge of the sink.

'Anything I can do?' he offered, but she waved him off with one hand while she reached for the roll of paper towel to stifle the paroxysm of coughing.

If only she didn't keep replaying his words inside her head she might have been able to catch her breath sooner. As it was, all she could hear was 'wouldn't it be a good idea if we went to bed?' playing over and over, and her body's intimate response telling her in no uncertain terms that it agreed.

Tired as she was, it was almost a relief when her mobile phone demanded her attention, signalling the need for yet another foray into the night.

She was stepping into her shoes by the front door when Nick spoke, his voice far too close for comfort as the husky words wrapped around her in the darkness.

'I actually meant that we should sleep in separate beds,' he said softly, and her cheeks suddenly felt as though they ought to be glowing. Could the wretched man read her mind? Was she that obvious?

'I'll be here when you get back, so don't worry about the girls,' he added, then waited until she was stepping out into the night before he finished in a voice edged with unexpected intensity. 'Drive carefully, Frankie. Come home safe.'

'Frankie, could I have a word with you?' said an uncertain voice behind her, and she turned to find Vicky standing there.

Instantly, guilt made her stomach clench tight, compounding the vague discomfort that had followed her all morning. She'd had yesterday off to catch up on her sleep after a very busy night on call but she still wasn't feeling right. If she was going down with this wretched flu…

'I know this is going to sound really strange, especially as we don't really know each other, but… well…Nick talks about your girls so much that we thought…well, it was Joe who suggested it, actually, but do you think they'd like to be bridesmaids?'

Frankie was startled by the unexpected invitation and didn't know what to think except that the feelings of guilt seemed to be growing with each day.

Vicky was such a lovely young woman, bright, intelligent and, by all accounts, excellent at her job. It was hardly her fault that the eight years difference in their ages seemed like a hundred years to Frankie, or that Frankie could hardly bear to look her in the face.

All she could think about each time she saw her was that she'd spent two unforgettable nights with the unsuspecting woman's fiancé.

'Joe suggested it?' she repeated in puzzlement, latching onto the first thing she thought of to stop the whirling tangle in her head.

What on earth did Joseph Faraday have to do with Nick's and Vicky's wedding arrangements? He was a fellow GP, but outside duty hours the widower usually kept himself very much to himself, behaving far more like an elderly recluse than a handsome thirty-seven-year-old.

'He came up to see one of his patients and we were talking over a cup of coffee,' Vicky explained hurriedly, the sudden flare of heat over her cheeks and the way she couldn't meet Frankie's eyes giving her an almost furtive air.

Takes one to know one, Frankie thought, wondering what else Vicky might have been talking about. At least her faithfulness to Nick wouldn't be in question, not after waiting twelve years for the man she loved.

'But wouldn't you rather choose attendants from among your friends and relations?' she asked, abandoning useless speculation to return the conversation to the original topic.

'That's rather the point,' the younger woman admitted. 'There aren't any young relatives to invite, and I didn't really want to have colleagues because otherwise I'd have to have at least a dozen of them if I didn't want to put any noses out of joint. Your two would solve the problem perfectly. Apart from the fact that Nick's become so fond of them, they're young enough to look pretty but old enough to be counted on to behave.'

'As the person who taught them their manners, I thank you,' Frankie said with a mock curtsey, but under cover of the joking she was trying to decide what to do.

Even if she'd been invited to the wedding, and as a member of the practice it was almost a given that she would be, she'd decided that she was going to find a cast-iron reason not to attend.

Her initial explosive attraction to Nick hadn't abated

in the least on closer acquaintance. In fact, if he hadn't been several years younger than herself and already engaged to Vicky, she might almost have entertained daydreams of marrying the man herself.

If she were to agree to Laura and Katie being bridesmaids, she would have no option but to be there, watching from the congregation while the man she craved with a hunger she'd never known before made his promises to another woman.

But if she turned the invitation down and Laura and Katie got to hear about it... Was she prepared for the fact that the two of them would probably never speak to her again?

Ever since Laura had been old enough to start school, she'd been coming home at intervals with excited news of the participation of yet another of her classmates in a wedding. Frankie hadn't a clue why both girls had become so enthralled with the idea. It had taken a long time for them to grasp the fact that, as the daughters of an only child, there would be no family wedding for them to serve in.

An invitation out of the blue to dress up in special clothes and be the centre of attention would be viewed as manna from heaven.

Was it guilt or just plain common sense that was urging caution? How did Nick feel about the idea and how could she find out without upsetting Vicky? She knew he got on well with the girls, but was he really happy to have them foisted on his wedding?

'I'm sure the two of them would be over the moon, but would you mind if I took a day or two to think about it?' she temporised uneasily. 'I know it's not a case of rent-a-kid, but as we're not related in any way to either family, and the girls don't know you...'

'I don't mind at all,' Vicky said with an understanding smile which incomprehensibly had Frankie gritting her teeth.

With her long blonde hair, blue eyes and perfect body, did Vicky Lawrence also have to be so *nice*?

'I can understand why you'd want to think about it, but I hope you don't mind if I keep my fingers crossed. Nick has told me what great kids they are.'

It was nearly an hour later that Frankie finally isolated something that had been niggling at the back of her memory ever since she'd spoken with Vicky.

Ultimately, it was an inconsequential thing, but for some reason it seemed very significant to her that it was the first time she'd heard the younger woman call Nick anything other than his old nickname, Johnny.

For some reason that left her feeling curiously unsettled, almost as though Vicky were talking about another man. For twelve years she'd been in love with Johnny, her childhood idol, and now she was planning her marriage to Nick.

Frankie shrugged. It wasn't really any of her business what they called each other, was it? All she had to do was come to a decision about her daughters' involvement in the celebration.

The fact that something inside her was rebelling at the very idea of having to watch the man making his vows to another woman was just another thing she was going to have to learn to live with.

'You're looking pensive, my dear,' said a dearly familiar voice, and she realised that Norman Castle had come into the room while she'd been sunk in her own thoughts.

'Trying to decide whether I'm just tired or if I'm going down with flu,' she retorted wearily. 'Why is it that although February is the shortest month, it always seems to drag on interminably.'

'I believe it's something to do with our bodies' depressive response to shorter hours of daylight,' he answered with the familiar air of pedantry that sometimes overtook him. 'Angela and I wanted to cheer everybody up with a bit of a party. We thought of throwing a belated engagement bash for Nick and Vicky, but almost as soon as we got rid of all the coach-crash victims we started with the flu epidemic, so it just hasn't been feasible.'

'That would have been nice,' she said, hoping she sounded more sincere than she felt. 'Perhaps you could do it when everything's back to normal.'

'There's no point if they're getting married only a few weeks later. I think we're going to have to think of another idea. See if you can come up with something that will lift all our spirits.'

'The only thing on my immediate horizon is Katie's tenth birthday at the end of the month.'

'Ten already?' he marvelled, sounding every bit like a proud surrogate grandfather. 'And how old is your younger one now? Seven, or is it eight?'

'Katie *is* the younger one,' she pointed out wryly. 'Laura is eleven. She'll be starting senior school in September.'

'Oh, my life, doesn't time pass so quickly?' he exclaimed. 'It doesn't seem but a minute ago that you arrived here with two little cherubs in tow.'

'And yet sometimes it feels like a million light years ago,' she countered. 'It feels almost as if I've always lived in Edenthwaite.'

'That's what we like to hear,' he said with beaming approval. 'Wait till you're my age and find that your younger patients are the third and fourth generation of the first ones you treated as a newcomer.'

Somehow, today, that prospect seemed more a cause for depression than something to look forward to, but Frankie wouldn't hurt his feelings by telling him so.

Still, there wasn't time to brood. In speaking about Katie's fast-approaching birthday, she'd reminded herself that she still had to plan what she was going to do to celebrate the event.

In the meantime, it was high time she took herself off to her consulting room because she had a full list of patients coming to see her this morning and another equally full of home visits for this afternoon. At this rate, by the time she finished it would probably be time for Laura and Katie to go to bed and far too late to discuss birthday plans.

'It comes to something when you have to write yourself a memo to talk to your daughter,' she muttered as she scribbled in her bulging diary. 'But with only a few days left to organise anything…'

The intercom buzzed to let her know that her first patient had arrived and she deliberately wiped thoughts of home and family out of her head. As tired as she was, it was going to need all her concentration to get through the day successfully. There was no way she wanted to let a lapse in attention be the cause of missing an important symptom.

'Hey, Mum!' Katie called brightly from the other side of the GP unit's waiting area.

Frankie gave a despairing glance at her watch and thanked God for her daughters' amenable natures. Her afternoon of visits had been extended by several extras so that she was now nearly an hour later than she should have been.

'I'm sorry I'm so late,' she called back as she gratefully dumped a pile of notes and files into the wire basket held out to her by receptionist Mara Frost.

'That's all right,' Laura piped up from her seat behind a rack of information leaflets. 'Dr Lawrence came to get us from school and everyone was looking at his car.'

'Then Nick's been helping us with our homework,' Katie added, oblivious to the sudden leap her mother's pulse gave at the mention of his name. 'I've asked him if he'll come with us for my birthday treat. I know it's supposed to be just for family but he's stayed at our house so that makes him sort of family, doesn't it? Is that all right?'

A movement behind the rack of leaflets resolved itself into the shape of Nick Johnson, straightening up from his position beside Laura.

'I told Katie that it was your decision,' he said quietly, the deep tones of his voice enough to set up an uncontrollable trembling somewhere at her core. It took her a moment to subdue it and find her voice.

'We haven't even discussed what she wants to do for her birthday,' Frankie replied weakly. 'It's a family tradition that the celebrant gets to choose a special treat that we can all share.'

'I explained that,' Katie said importantly, almost bouncing up and down with excitement. 'And I've decided what I want us to do—go horse-riding.'

Frankie remembered that she'd wanted to do the same thing last year but the foot-and-mouth epidemic raging at the time had prevented the outing from happening.

'And you're willing to go?' she asked, finally daring to meet his eyes. The jolt of recognition was faster and harder than ever. Just one look at that deep blue gaze and she could tell that he still wanted her every bit as much as she wanted him.

'Only on condition that the girls promise to take care of me,' he said with an apprehensive look that she was certain he was putting on for the girls' benefit.

'Don't worry, Nick,' Katie said kindly. 'We've been before so we can tell you what to do. And the horses are very good. They're so big that they look frightening but they're really very gentle.'

'In which case, I'd be delighted to accept your invitation,' he said with a courtly bow that made both girls giggle. 'Get your mum to tell me where and when and I'll make sure to be there.'

'And you'll have to come back afterwards to have some birthday cake, won't he, Mum?' Laura finished, turning to Frankie with a beseeching expression.

'Chocolate cake?' Nick asked.

What could Frankie do but agree? Although the third hopeful expression ranged beside Laura's and Katie's almost made her laugh aloud.

The urge to laugh was what stuck so vividly in her mind that she was still thinking about it hours later. It was something she'd done far too little of, over the last few years, but ever since she'd met Nick…

Was 'met' the right word? she debated silently in the quiet of her room, covers pulled right up to her ears against the February chill of a double bed with only one occupant. Nick's advent into her life had been far too explosive to be called a mere meeting.

Whatever it was, his presence seemed to have made so many things different, and this time she wasn't thinking about the burden of guilt sitting on her conscience.

The urge to laugh aloud might have been the trigger but, now that she thought about it, even her current feeling of exhaustion hadn't curbed the deep certainty that she was doing the right job in the right place. It didn't matter that spring might still be many weeks away, she found herself noticing the stark grandeur of her surroundings with a more appreciative eye than usual.

Even her overwhelming concern about her ex-husband's threat to take the children to live with him didn't seem such a worry these days. It was nearly a month since he'd made his announcement and she'd heard nothing. Knowing what a legal shark he could be, she would have expected something to have happened by now, so perhaps he'd changed his mind.

In fact, if it weren't for the minor detail that Nick was preparing to marry another woman, Frankie was pretty certain that her life hadn't been this good since…well, she couldn't remember when. Still, she'd been quite content with her largely solitary life for the last seven years, and she'd always known that Nick could never be hers. It was up to the two of them to find a way to work together amicably while they got on with their lives.

In her new state of optimism, even that seemed a relatively simple task.

As the bed grew warmer she began to relax towards sleep. She was happily basking in the unexpected feeling of well-being when a little voice in the back of her head intruded with an unwelcome reminder.

If something seems too good to be true, it probably is, it whispered, sending a sharp shiver of apprehension the length of her spine.

CHAPTER SEVEN

SATURDAY dawned bright and dry but very cold.

Frankie glared at the clock beside the bed and pulled the covers up over her nose, hoping for just a few more minutes, but from the sounds along the hallway that wasn't likely.

'Happy birthday to you...' she heard Laura singing.

Katie chimed in with, 'Happy birthday to *me*!'

She gave a resigned sigh, knowing that the day had officially started. There would be no leisurely lie-in today.

At least Laura and Katie were happy and got along with each other reasonably well. She'd had so many children in her consulting room who did nothing but argue with each other that she knew she had grounds for counting herself lucky.

She took a bracing breath and flung the covers back then forced herself to climb straight out.

For several seconds the room seemed to sway around her and she was afraid she was going to be sick.

Sitting shakily down again, she leant forward, instinct as much as her medical training telling her to bring her head closer to the level of her heart.

'Not flu. Not today,' she groaned, thinking of all the things she still had to do today to make Katie's day perfect.

Several deep breaths later she gingerly straightened up again, relieved to find that her surroundings were behaving themselves again. Her stomach still felt a little less certain, but that could be a combination of hunger, excitement and the underlying stress of the custody situation and her guilt over Nick.

There was a hollow thud in the hallway below, followed by a squeal from the two girls as they emerged from Katie's room to go thundering down the stairs.

'Mum! The postman's been,' Katie announced gleefully on her way past her mother's door, clearly already enjoying every minute of her special day.

Frankie silently had to admit that this was the first of her daughters' birthdays that she'd been looking forward to in her own right. She'd always loved doing those extra little things for her girls—baking a special cake or organising a particular outing. But this time Nick would be sharing the day with them and although he'd been invited by Katie, somehow her brain was having trouble fighting the notion that he was there for her benefit.

'Mum! I've got cards! They're addressed to me!' Katie shouted, the exclamation marks almost visible in the air in her excitement.

'You'd better hurry up and get dressed, then,' Frankie called back.

'But, Mu-u-m...' Katie wailed. 'I want to open them *now*!'

'Breakfast rules,' Frankie said, reminding her of the family tradition that, Christmas, Easter or birthdays, any cards or gifts were only opened after breakfast was over.

'But, Mu-u-m!' she tried cajoling again, but Frankie wouldn't budge. That little breathing space had saved many an argument and she wasn't going to break the ritual now.

'If you're in that much of a hurry, you'd better get

upstairs and decide what you want to wear,' she pointed out firmly. 'You don't want Nick to arrive before you're dressed, do you?'

'Come on, Katie,' she heard Laura mutter. 'She wouldn't let me open mine either. Let's get dressed.'

Frankie smiled, pleased she'd stuck her ground. The last thing she wanted to do was let either of her girls think they were being treated better or worse than the other. Their open love for each other was something too precious to spoil with sibling rivalry.

Breakfast was one of their favourites in winter, traditional south-of-the-border porridge made with milk and a sprinkle of brown sugar over the top. In honour of the day there was a swirl of thin cream, too.

Frankie had to stifle a chuckle when both girls were in too much of a hurry to see what the post had brought to volunteer to do the washing-up, but she took pity on them.

'I'll do it while you bring the post to the table,' she told Katie. 'Laura, would you go to my dressing-table and bring down the things I've left there, please?'

Katie might have graduated to double figures in her age, but it didn't mean she'd grown any less openly enthusiastic in her reactions.

Each card brought exclamations of pleasure and Frankie was pleased to see that even Martin's sister had remembered her niece this year.

Bearing in mind that they'd be seeing him shortly, she was surprised to see that Katie had a card from Nick, too. How could a bachelor, who admitted to almost no experience with children, know how much the gesture would mean to a ten-year-old? And as for the book token he'd enclosed, it was more than her own father had done for her.

Eventually, all the cards were arranged to Katie's satisfaction along the mantelpiece and she was just twirling around to model her new fleece jacket when they heard the sound of Nick's car.

'Nick, come and look,' Katie called, only prevented from leaping out onto the front path in her socks by a hasty grab of the back of her new jacket. 'Thank you so much for the book token,' she added as soon as he entered the hallway, flinging her arms around his waist in an exuberant hug.

For a moment he seemed totally nonplussed by her actions, both hands hovering uncertainly above her shoulders as he glanced towards Frankie as if for guidance.

Frankie just grinned at him and felt the prick of tears when he wrapped one arm gently around her daughter's shoulders and cradled her head in the other.

'You're very welcome, Katie,' he said in an emotionally husky voice as he tentatively stroked her dark shiny hair. 'Happy birthday, sunshine.'

'Come and see her cards, Nick. She's got loads of them,' Laura invited.

Of course, then he had to see Katie's presents, too, and, knowing just how long that could take, Frankie silently took herself off to make the poor man a cup of coffee.

Catching sight of herself in the bright surface of the kettle, she realised that her face was wreathed in an idiotic smile.

She paused to stare at the image, wondering just how long it had been since she'd last caught herself smiling over nothing, smiling just because it felt as if everything was right with her world.

'Uh-uh.' She shook her head and turned away from

the tell-tale sign. She did not need a man to make her happy. She'd made that mistake before and had ended up very unhappy.

Anyway, Nick wasn't in her life in that way. He was only spending part of the day with them to celebrate Katie's birthday. There was nothing personal in it at all.

'Here, Nick,' she said as she offered him the steaming mug. 'You should just about have time to finish that before it's time to go. And as for you two, you need to get your things together. Gloves, boots…'

She was speaking to their backs as they ran out of the room and for just a second she wondered when scientists would find a way to bottle children's excess energy. She could do with some.

'Have they got all the proper gear?' Nick asked as he leant one elbow on the mantelpiece and sipped his coffee.

'They wish!' Frankie rolled her eyes. 'I was the idiot who suggested this as an outing the first time and I think they're well on the way to being hooked. At the moment we hire hats and body protectors at the stable but I've a feeling that life is going to get very expensive in the near future, and not just in financial terms.'

'Would you rather they didn't ride?'

'Not at all. It's just… Can you imagine what a logistic nightmare it would be? It's bad enough trying to co-ordinate my timetable with their visitation rota. How would I add in regular riding lessons? Then, in September, Laura moves up to senior school and she'll have the option of all sorts of after-school activities— music, sports, drama… Next year, it'll be Katie's turn to move up and I'll be so busy racing round organising the two of them and their social calendar that I won't even have time to go to work any more.'

And the wretched man had the nerve to laugh.

For a fraction of a second she almost succumbed to anger but then her sense of humour kicked in.

'Just you wait,' she warned with a narrow-eyed glare that only set him chuckling again. 'I'll get my own back. We'll see who's laughing when you're so stiff after the horse-riding that you're walking like John Wayne.'

At that point the girls came thundering back down the stairs full of excited chatter and it was time to go.

'Hey, Katie, are you *sure* you don't want to swap?' Nick wheedled as he stood beside her to give her a leg-up onto the pretty grey pony she'd been assigned.

'No!' She giggled as she settled herself into the saddle. 'You're too big. Your legs would reach the ground if you got on Misty.'

'What a good idea!' he exclaimed. 'I think my horse is half-giraffe. My legs will never reach the ground on him.'

For all Nick's rude comments, the animal he was to ride was a beauty, and far more his size than a child's pony.

Suddenly Frankie was assailed with a terrible feeling of guilt. What if he really *was* afraid? Horses were large animals and some people were genuinely frightened of them. The poor man had more or less been railroaded into coming by her daughters. How could she give him a way out without spoiling their pleasure in the day's treat?

She watched while he gave Laura her share of atten-

tion and saw the extra self-confidence in her posture
after his quiet words of praise.

He was going to make a wonderful father one of
these days, she thought, and the tight pain around her
heart almost robbed her of breath.

In the blink of an eye there were so many emotions
whirling round inside her that she could hardly sort
them out.

There was pleasure and gratitude that he was doing
his best to make Katie's birthday special and there was
sadness mixed with more than a hint of jealousy that
it was just a temporary situation. All too soon he was
going to be marrying Vicky, and who knew how long
it would be before he was taking his own children out
for their first lessons on horseback?

The most painful emotion was the realisation that
she was falling in love with the man and that it was
going to cause her nothing but misery.

'Nick, it's your turn now,' Katie called, snapping
Frankie out of her churning thoughts to the awareness
that she'd left it too late to rescue Nick with his dignity
intact. He was already standing beside that sleekly
powerful animal and preparing to mount it.

It wasn't until she concentrated on what he was doing that she realised that he was actually standing on
the wrong side of the animal but when she would have
pointed out his error she was treated to a surreptitious
wink.

Silenced, she watched while he clambered aboard,
knowing from her own childhood how awkward it
could be—almost as impossible as a right-hander trying
to use scissors with their left hand.

Katie and Laura were so busy praising him for getting into the saddle that they didn't notice that he

needed no assistance to check the length of his stirrups or how to hold the reins. Frankie saw, and knew that this was far from the first time he'd been riding. At least that was one thing she could stop feeling guilty about.

'OK, John Wayne. Smile for the camera,' Frankie instructed, stepping back far enough to get all three of them in the frame, then finishing with an individual picture of each of them.

She waved as they set off for the instruction arena, following at a safe distance to watch and take more shots as the lesson progressed.

Next time, perhaps she should think about joining in, too. It was many years since she'd last ridden but if Nick was game to give it another go, why shouldn't she? Perhaps they could go for a hack out into the countryside together once she'd rediscovered her old skills.

Except there wouldn't be a next time, not with Laura and Katie or with Frankie...not unless Vicky was a rider, and even then, why would she want to have another woman and her children tagging along?

'Enough!' she scolded herself, opting to sit in the protection of Nick's car to watch when her feet started to turn to ice. 'This is Katie's day and you're only going to think happy thoughts.'

And those thoughts included Nick's company for a fast-food lunch—another birthday tradition that usually ended up as a choice between hamburgers and pizza— and then home again for the promised chocolate cake.

'Frankie, I've got a bone to pick with you,' Vicky announced on Monday morning for all the world to hear.

Well, it wasn't quite all the world, just the half-dozen or so who happened to be within earshot at the time. Still, if the rumour machine was working as well as ever, that meant her words were going to be all round Edenthwaite in about half a nanosecond.

The morning had started off badly and looked as if it was only going to get worse, Frankie thought with a silent groan as she felt the guilty blush spread up her throat and into her cheeks.

The girls had been cranky this morning, probably caused by the feeling of let-down at the end of an exciting weekend. Or perhaps they were incubating this same flu bug that she'd been fighting for the last couple of days.

Now it looked as if Vicky had found out about her liaisons with Nick and was going to confront her with the knowledge.

'A bone?' she questioned, uncomfortably aware that there was a very un-doctor-like quiver to her voice. She'd never had a confrontation like this with another woman, not even when she'd discovered Martin's infidelity.

'Yes. Ever since Saturday, Nick's been raving about that chocolate birthday cake you made, so I think that the very least you can do is let me have a copy of the recipe.'

Relief lent a sharp edge to Frankie's laughter.

'No problem,' she agreed, feeling distinctly light-headed. 'That was actually the teetotal version for junior birthdays. There are a couple of adult versions with brandy or cherries soaked in kirsch in them.'

'Don't tell me any more,' Vicky begged. 'I'm a complete chocoholic and they sound so decadent that my mouth's watering. By the way, Jack and I had fun yes-

terday teasing him about walking like John Wayne.
Apparently it's been years since he last went riding.'

With a cheery wave she hurried off in the direction
of the lifts, on her way to her domain in the north wing.

Frankie leant weakly against the nearest wall, feeling
rather as if she'd just been on a roller-coaster ride.

One minute she was expecting to be denounced as
a man-eater, the next she was being asked for a favourite recipe, then being thanked for giving everyone
a laugh at Nick's expense.

There hadn't been a word about the fact that she'd
appropriated a fiancé, or about the fact that Frankie still
hadn't made a decision about Laura's and Katie's involvement in the wedding ceremony.

And her head was spinning again.

'Nick! You tell her it'll be all right,' Laura appealed.
'She won't listen to me.'

Frankie managed not to groan aloud but it was a
close thing.

This argument had been raging for several days now,
and she'd actually agreed to Katie inviting Nick to join
them for supper in the mistaken impression that it
would stop Laura raising the topic.

No such luck.

Ever since her daughter had heard that the senior
school Valentine's Day disco, postponed by the coach
crash, had been rescheduled for this Friday evening,
she'd been agitating to be allowed to attend.

The fact that she wasn't yet a member of the school
wasn't a bar, as the event had been planned as a local
fund-raiser with a minimum age of eleven.

Frankie was almost certain that her objections had
nothing to do with the fact that it would be just one

more piece of evidence that her babies were growing up fast.

Her main objection, and the one that she couldn't mention to Laura, was that it was due to take place on a weekend she was supposed to spend with her father. She had no idea what Martin's attitude might be to the idea of his daughter attending such an event and she wasn't about to stir him up into pursuing his intention of applying for custody if he'd allowed the idea to die.

She did know that although *he'd* often changed custody weekends with very little notice, he objected most strongly if she wanted to make any alterations in the schedule.

That didn't mean that she would necessarily have given Laura her permission if the event had happened at another time, or that she was willing to allow an eleven-year-old to stay out late, albeit to a well-supervised event. At the moment, she didn't want to give him any excuse, no matter how trivial, to be able to claim that she wasn't a fit mother.

Unfortunately, all Laura could see was that her mother was being an unreasonable killjoy.

'I'm already eleven and lots of my friends will be going,' Laura was saying, rehashing the arguments that Frankie had grown heartily sick of over the last few days. 'Will you have a word with her, Nick, and persuade her to let me go?'

'Uh-uh!' Nick shook his head and raised both hands defensively. 'I'm not getting in the middle of a private war. This is strictly between you and your mother.'

'But, Nick! She'd listen if you talked to her,' Laura pleaded. 'You think I'm old enough to go, don't you? And there'll be plenty of parents supervising as well as all the teachers. Please!'

'I'm sorry, Laura, but it's not right,' he said gently. 'I'm your friend and your mother's friend and it wouldn't be fair for me to side with either of you.'

'That means you're siding with her.' She pouted, her face set in an uncharacteristically mulish expression. 'When I was talking to you before, you said I had to make my own choices so that they'd be right for me. Where's the point if I'm not allowed to do what I've decided? It's my first grown-up disco and she won't let me go and it's not fair!'

She whirled round and flounced out of the room, her progress marked by heavy feet storming up the stairs and the slam of her bedroom door.

Frankie sighed. 'I'm sorry about that. I honestly thought she'd put a lid on it if you were here but it just seems to have made it worse.'

'She thinks it's the grown-ups ganging up against her?' he suggested. 'I'm sorry if I've complicated things. Would you rather I left?'

'Certainly not!' Frankie said hastily, not wanting to give up the chance of spending time with him even if it was completely chaperoned by two eagle-eyed daughters—*especially* if it was chaperoned by those eagle-eyed daughters.

That way lay safety. There was no chance of anything getting out of hand.

Anyway, she wanted a chance to ask him about that 'making choices' comment Laura had made, and she couldn't do that with Katie's ears wagging.

'You were invited to share a meal with us, Nick. Do you want to help Katie set the table?'

Laura was a very sulky presence at the table in spite of Nick's best efforts and Frankie was afraid he was going to want to leave as soon as the meal was over, leaving her no time for a quiet word.

She hadn't realised that he was second on call that night until his phone rang just as he was helping the girls to clear the table at the end of the first course.

'I'm sorry, Frankie,' he said as he switched off the mobile. 'This is going to seem like a clever ploy so that I can eat and run, but I'm going to have to go.'

'But you haven't had pudding yet,' Katie pointed out, clearly aghast at the prospect.

'If I finish my call soon enough, I could come back for it later, if your mother doesn't mind,' he suggested. 'Do you know what it is?' he added in a stage whisper. 'Is it worth my while, coming back?'

'Apple crumble and custard,' Katie whispered back behind her hand.

'Definitely worth coming back for,' he agreed. 'I can't remember when I last had apple crumble. Probably when I was at school.'

'But that's years and years!' she exclaimed, totally forgetting to whisper in her horror. 'You've probably forgotten what it tastes like.'

The wry expression on his face made Frankie chuckle. She could have told him that her daughter believed that anyone beyond their teenage years was already heading for senile dementia at a rapid rate.

The fact that Nick might be returning at any minute somehow made Laura's surly mood more bearable.

Clearly her daughter was intelligent enough to realise that as plan A—verbal persuasion—and plan B—enlisting outside help, had both failed, it was time to try plan C—sulking.

She wasn't to know that it didn't matter how many letters of the alphabet she tried, the answer was always going to be the same. Frankie didn't dare to upset Martin for fear that he would carry through his intention of applying for custody.

Once the girls went up to have their baths and get ready for bed she had a few moments to herself. With a sigh of relief she sat down with a cup of tea and put her feet up. Unfortunately, that didn't mean that she could switch her mind off, and the only way to stop herself listening for the sound of Nick's return like a star-struck schoolgirl was to replay some of the problems she'd encountered during the day.

Actually, there was only one patient who really stuck in her mind, a sixteen-year-old pupil at the school where the disco was due to be held.

For just a moment, Frankie wondered if her adamant refusal to allow Laura to attend the event had anything to do with Ann Timothy's situation, and couldn't be absolutely sure.

Her first visit to the practice had been a month or so ago, brought by her mother for some help with a persistent sore throat.

When a course of antibiotics hadn't helped, Frankie had swabbed her throat and sent the sample off to be cultured for identification.

Today, the pretty youngster had attended on her own, obviously expecting to be handed a prescription for a more specific antibiotic to solve her problem.

Frankie could still see the youngster's pretty face in her mind's eye when she'd sat down in the chair beside her to break the news.

'Ann, the results are back from the lab,' she began gently, 'and I'm afraid they show that you've got a sexually transmitted disease.'

'W-what? B-but that's impossible,' she stammered,

her face going white with shock then red with embarrassment.

'I'm afraid it's true,' Frankie insisted. 'You've been diagnosed with gonorrhoea.'

'But I haven't... We didn't... I'm still a virgin,' she finished, clearly mortified to be speaking about this with an adult.

'But you have had oral sex, haven't you?'

'Only once,' she admitted with a grimace. 'It was gross, but I didn't want to risk getting pregnant so... Oh, God, you mean I've got gonorrhoea in my *throat*!'

'You'll need to inform your boyfriend so he can be tested and treated, and both of you will have to tell any other partners so they can be tested, too.'

'Oh...my...God,' she breathed, her pale blue eyes widening with every word. 'Everyone will know.'

'Not if you do it discreetly on a one-to-one basis. And you can't duck out of it,' Frankie reminded her sternly, hating to have to appear so severe when the girl was still clearly shocked. 'I'm afraid it's one of the tougher parts of being an adult—facing up to your responsibilities. I can give you an injection now that should solve the problem, but in future it would be a good idea if you started practising safe sex.'

'I thought we were,' her patient muttered glumly as she prepared for the injection of ceftriaxone, apparently becoming resigned to the situation.

'There's also a chance that you might have been infected with *Chlamydia*, which is more difficult to diagnose than gonorrhoea, so I want you to take a week's course of doxycycline to be certain.'

She went to the computer to print off a prescription while Ann straightened her clothes, then turned to face her to deliver her final warning.

'Listen, Ann. I know this has all come as a shock and it's all going to be a bit embarrassing over the next few weeks but it really is important for you to take this seriously. Not only will you make certain that your friends aren't at risk of passing this around, but you're also safeguarding everybody's future.'

'Our futures? How?'

Frankie was glad to see that she'd caught the young-ster's attention.

'Well, everybody's heard about Aids and VD and have a pretty good idea of what they involve, but very few know that if a girl contracts a Chlamydia infection it can make her sterile.'

'Sterile!' That almost seemed to have shocked her more than the news that she'd caught gonorrhoea.

'So,' Frankie continued, 'you can see how important it is that *anyone* who might have been in contact should get themselves checked out, or you could end up with a whole class full of female friends who can never have any children.'

'It's enough to put you off sex for life,' Ann mut-tered. 'Is it really worth all the hassle?'

'It is if you find the right partner,' Frankie reassured her. 'How about waiting a bit longer before you start getting serious?'

'You mean, use my mouth for talking instead?' she challenged with a glint in her eyes that told Frankie that this was probably one young woman who was go-ing to be able to use this setback to make her stronger.

'A good plan,' Frankie agreed with a grin. 'You'll probably find that the…ah…*sexual equipment* of the men worth knowing isn't nearly as sexy as their minds.'

* * *

The girls were ready for bed by the time she recognised the sound of Nick's four-by-four reversing into the drive.

'Mu-u-m!' called a voice from the top of the stairs. 'Can Nick come up to say goodnight?'

She should have known that Katie's sharp ears would pick his arrival up, too. It still went against the grain to hear her daughters call the man by his first name, but that was a fight she'd lost right at the beginning when Nick had insisted that he preferred it to being called 'Uncle' as a courtesy title.

She opened the back door before he could knock and was greeted with a smile that warmed her right through.

'I take it the offer of apple crumble is still open?' he asked as he stepped into the warmth of the kitchen, bringing with him the sharp scent of the chilly night.

'I'll serve some out if you'll stick your head round Katie's door to say goodnight,' she bargained. 'Would you like tea or coffee to go with it?'

'Coffee, please,' he said with a grimace. 'I'm going to need it if I'm going to have to stay awake tonight.'

Frankie kept one ear on the soft sound of voices upstairs while she retrieved from the fridge the man-sized portion of crumble she'd saved for him. It wouldn't take a moment to nuke it in the microwave and if she whisked a little single cream into the custard and heated that through, they would still be better than anything shop-bought.

Finally the small cafetière was ready, too, and still Nick hadn't returned.

Knowing how likely it was that Katie would be trying to talk him into telling her yet more of his 'politically correct' fairy stories, she set off with a smile to rescue him.

To her surprise, Katie's light was off and there wasn't a sound coming from her room. It was Laura's light that was on.

The voices were too soft for her to be able to pick out the words, so at least her daughter wasn't shouting at him.

Tentatively, Frankie tapped on the door with her fingertips and pushed it open a little further.

'Is everything all right?' she asked when she saw the serious expressions on both their faces.

Laura was sitting up in bed with her chin propped on her knees with her bedclothes draped over the top like a bulky tent. Nick had turned the plain wooden chair round from the desk where she sometimes worked on her homework projects, and was sitting astride it with his arms folded on the back rail.

'Everything's fine,' Nick assured her with a quick smile.

'I apologised for being rude,' Laura announced, rather more belligerently. 'It's not *his* fault that you don't want me to grow up.'

'Laura!' Frankie exclaimed, hurt by her attitude but still unwilling to explain the reasons for her decision.

Her daughter was only eleven and the last thing she wanted to do was put her in the middle of a tug of war between her parents. That would probably cause far more psychological damage than missing one school disco.

'Laura,' Nick said, the word sounding almost like a warning, and to Frankie's surprise, Laura subsided almost instantly.

'Sorry,' she muttered with a sideways glance, and

slid down the bed to lie with the covers pulled right up to her nose. 'I need to go to sleep now,' she added, and turned her back on both of them.

Defeated, Frankie whispered goodnight and led the way out of the room. Tears were threatening so she left Nick to turn out the light, using the time spent going back to the kitchen to get herself under control.

'Are you sure you don't want me to go away?' he offered as soon as he joined her.

'No. Please,' she said hastily, gesturing towards the place she'd set for him. She'd almost resigned herself to the fact that he'd only suggested breaking his engagement when he'd been worried that she might be pregnant. He certainly hadn't mentioned it again.

'It would be nice to have a few moments of adult conversation while you finish that. The last couple of days it's been a bit like living in the middle of a battlefield. I've hardly dared open my mouth without having the conversation turned into yet another reason why she should be allowed to go to this wretched disco and why I'm such an awful mother for refusing permission.'

'And the real reason?' he prompted before he put the first spoonful of dessert in his mouth.

'Martin,' she said distractedly, then forced herself to tear her eyes away from his mouth as it closed over the cutlery. She wasn't surprised that he realised there would be a good reason for her decision, but she was pleased that he knew her well enough to predict it.

'Mmm. Fantastic!' he groaned through the mouthful as his eyes drifted closed with every appearance of ecstasy.

Frankie was stunned by the bolt of desire that hit her. He'd looked just like that when they'd…

'I've never tasted crumble like this before,' he continued, almost drooling as he loaded the spoon again. 'You've put some spice in it, haven't you?'

'Cinnamon, and a little brown sugar,' she told him, mesmerised by his whole-hearted enjoyment of the simple dish. It was just more evidence, if she'd needed it, that he was a man who seemed to enjoy his senses to the full.

'Sorry to sidetrack you. You were saying about Martin?' he prompted, dragging her back to far less pleasant thoughts.

'Yes. Martin.' She sighed. 'Unfortunately, the disco takes place on a weekend the girls are due to spend with their father.'

'And he wouldn't agree to swap weekends?'

'I don't even want to ask,' she said bluntly. 'I haven't heard anything further about his decision to have the custody agreement changed, so just in case he's having second thoughts, I don't want to do anything to rock the boat.'

'Didn't Laura understand your reasoning?' He was already scraping the last of the dessert from the bowl as though he would clean the pattern off it, too.

'I haven't told her.'

'Why not? She's an intelligent girl. I'm sure she'd see it was—'

'I don't *want* her to have to understand,' Frankie broke in heatedly. 'I don't want to be one of those ex-wives who spends all her time bad-mouthing her husband. I might not love him or respect him any more, but he is still their father.'

It wasn't until he put his hand over hers that she realised she'd been twisting a teaspoon round and round between her fingers.

'Hey, I understand,' he assured her softly. 'And I admire you for it. Most women would leap on the chance to make their ex look bad.'

The look in Nick's eyes was only compounding the warmth flowing from his hand into hers and if she didn't do something *now*, the fact that there were two young girls upstairs wasn't going to make a scrap of difference to what happened down here.

'I just hope that in the end it's worth all the heartache,' she said quietly, reluctant to break the contact between them but knowing it had to be done.

'Time I went,' he said, his voice sounding as raw as her nerves as he pushed his chair back from the table and stood.

'Thanks for collecting the girls from school—again. And for running interference with Laura.'

'You're welcome, Frankie,' he said as he thrust his arms into his sleeves. 'Even when they're not behaving perfectly, I still think your two are great. I'm quite envious.'

'Well, it won't be too long before you can get started on some of your own,' she said brightly, looking up just in time to surprise a strange expression in his eyes.

'Maybe,' he said cryptically as he reached for the door.

He had one hand on the handle when, with a muttered imprecation, he whirled back towards her, his head already angled to meet hers as his arms encircled her startled body.

CHAPTER EIGHT

NICK had tasted of coffee and cinnamon and too many dreams that could never come true, Frankie thought as she hurried in the direction of the accident and emergency department the next morning.

Just one touch of his mouth on hers and she'd been ready to abandon all trace of restraint, wanting nothing more than to wrap her arms around him and welcome him into her body.

The trouble was, this time she knew absolutely that what she felt for him wasn't just an overwhelming physical attraction. She was in love with him, heart and soul, and it had probably happened the first time she'd seen him, standing there dripping wet. She would never be able to forget the expression in those beautiful blue eyes as he'd looked her over, as if she was more tempting than any chocolate cake and he was greedy to devour her one sweet morsel at a time.

In the end it had been love that had enabled her to draw back from the brink.

Frankie would have loved nothing more than to have taken him to her bed and loved the night away, even with her impressionable daughters in the same house, but she wasn't going to allow it to happen. She loved him too much to let him compromise his honour.

'No more, Nick,' she whispered, one finger pressed to his lips when he would have kissed her again. 'This mustn't happen any more.'

'You don't want it to happen?' he challenged huskily

with a telling glance towards the way her body was still tightly pressed against his.

'That's the trouble. I *do* want it to happen, but it can't. It's not fair to Vicky. It's not fair to *any* of us.'

She forced herself to take the step that would put space between the two of them, knowing she wouldn't be able to find the words she needed if they were touching.

'This is going to have to stop before people get hurt,' she said, trying to sound firm when her heart was already breaking. 'I'm very grateful that you've been willing to fetch the girls from school and that you've humoured them by accepting their invitations to meals and birthday treats, but they're getting too attached to you. They won't understand when you don't have time for them any more.'

'You don't want me to see them any more?' he demanded roughly, and she could have sworn that there was pain in his eyes. 'You want to cut off any association between us just like that?'

'It would probably be for the best,' she agreed softly, throwing a worried glance towards the door leading to the hallway and hoping that their voices wouldn't carry as far as the bedrooms. 'Once you're married to Vicky you'll be going home rather than sitting in the reception area, supervising their homework. You'll be having your meals with her and spending your weekends with her.'

'Anyone would think you were jealous,' he accused, his tone heated even though his expression was stony.

'Yes. In a way, I *am* jealous,' she admitted, opting for a partial truth even though she couldn't tell him of her love. 'I…*We*'ve enjoyed spending time with you. Sometimes it's been almost as if we were a real family.

Martin left them so long ago that Laura and Katie can't remember what that was like, but they've now got an idea of what they've been missing.'

'And you've had a taste or two of what *you*'ve been missing,' he pointed out cuttingly. 'Did you enjoy that, too?'

It distressed her that he would try to denigrate what they'd found in each other's arms, but if he was hurting even a fraction as much as she was, she could forgive him.

'Yes, I enjoyed it,' she admitted, refusing to look away from the accusation in his eyes even though her own were burning with the threat of tears. 'But I lo— I respect you too much to try to hang onto something that isn't right for any of us.'

'What gives you the right to make all the decisions?' he demanded harshly, his frustration showing as he speared his fingers through his hair. 'How do you know it isn't right?'

'Because it *can't* be,' she snapped back, suddenly reaching the end of her tether. 'I'm a divorced older woman who's already had one run-in with a man who didn't mind cheating on me. I'm already heading towards middle age with two almost-teenage daughters and a possible custody fight on my hands. And while you might want to carry on a temporary red-hot affair, you're not free to do anything about any of it.'

Nick left after that, closing the door so quietly behind him that it was somehow more telling than if he'd slammed it, hard.

She spent a wretched night, uselessly trying to find some alternative to banishing him from her life when she knew there wasn't one.

The air at the breakfast table was almost poisonous

with Laura's realisation that even her sulking hadn't persuaded her mother to change her mind about the disco. Even Katie was subdued, not even producing her usual groan when Frankie reminded her to leave her things ready to go to her father's that night.

At least she had a weekend to herself to look forward to, Frankie consoled herself. With any luck she'd catch up on some of her sleep and be over this wretched bug by the time the girls returned on Sunday night.

In the meantime, she had a patient waiting for her in the accident and emergency department. According to the message passed on to the GP unit, Joe needed someone to come and help him deal with a dislocated shoulder, and Frankie was the first one available.

To her surprise, it was Vicky waiting with the patient in the treatment room, and the patient was Joe Faraday himself, stripped to the waist and looking thoroughly miserable.

'Joe! What on earth happened to you?' Automatically she registered that his face was grey and pinched with pain and she couldn't miss the way he was cradling his arm against his naked chest.

'Fight with a bullock,' he muttered through clenched teeth.

'Some bullocks got out onto the road and he was putting them back into the field. One of them didn't want to go,' Vicky elaborated swiftly.

Her manner was almost nervous, but that was something Frankie didn't have time to ponder. The obvious deformity of the joint and the way he was protecting it were telling their own story. The ball joint had come out of the shoulder socket and could even now be pinching nerves or blood vessels. If they weren't released quickly, permanent damage could be done.

Frankie began a gentle palpation to establish the precise direction of the dislocation, hoping that there would be no signs of fracture, and was interrupted by Vicky.

'When I checked, his distal pulse was strong and there didn't seem to be any nerve deficit,' she said helpfully, removing two of Frankie's main concerns.

'Happened before,' Joe muttered, stifling a groan as Frankie inadvertently increased his discomfort during her examination.

'Frequently?' she demanded, knowing that a shoulder that recurrently dislocated was a different matter altogether. That might need surgery to make it stay where it belonged.

'Once. Playing rugby at med school. No trouble since.' The staccato delivery was enough to tell her the degree of pain and Frankie reached for a mask.

'Time to get this show on the road, then,' she said cheerfully. 'Start taking some good steady breaths while we get you comfortable and into position and then we'll reassemble you.'

Vicky took the mask out of her hand to settle it over Joe's face and even while she was contacting Trish to notify her they were going to need an X-ray, Frankie couldn't help noticing the gentle way she helped their patient to lie back on the couch.

'Do you need any help in here, or shall I go?' Nick announced, drawing their attention to his presence as he came into the room. 'It looks as if you've already got half the hospital staff in here.'

'It doesn't count if one of them is the patient,' Frankie announced, and turned back to Joe, but the fact

JOSIE METCALFE   139

that she wasn't looking at Nick didn't stop her awareness of him as he drew close behind her. 'Would you
rather pull or manipulate?'

'If you're feeling strong, you can pull,' Nick directed
as he stepped up beside the couch. 'How's the anaes-
thesia going, Vicky? Has he had enough to give birth
yet?'

There was a muffled growl from behind the mask
that translated to something roughly the equivalent of
'Stop making jokes and get on with it'.

Frankie couldn't help responding to the rueful grin
Nick sent her way, then it was time to concentrate on
the job in hand.

She moved Joe's arm gently until she was certain
that the Entonox had deadened the pain sufficiently,
then she moved it until it was pointing sideways from
his shoulder and locked her hands around his wrist.

'Ready?' she asked as Nick positioned himself in the
angle between Joe's arm and his body, his thumbs positioned on the protruding ball of the misplaced joint.

'Ready,' he confirmed, and Frankie began to pull.

She hadn't realised that Joe was quite so fit and well
muscled. In fact, she'd hardly noticed very much about
him at all as he seemed to make a habit of fading pretty
much into the background. She certainly knew that he
must be doing some form of regular exercise to keep
himself in such good shape, and it was those strong
muscles that were making her job so difficult at the
moment.

It was all very well having well-toned muscles
around the shoulder joint, but when they were actively
locking the component parts *out* of joint it was a different matter.

'We're going to need to swap jobs,' Frankie admitted when she couldn't get quite enough traction to pull the arm back into position. 'I think Joe must have been working out on the sly to get muscles like these.'

It was one thing to change places so they could get the job done. It was another thing entirely to have to squeeze past Nick between the couch and his body without rubbing up against every inch of him like an over-friendly cat. And under Vicky's gaze, too.

Frankie was glad to have to bend forward to concentrate on her new task but almost wished that she had long hair to hide the heat that had bloomed in her cheeks.

'Ready?' Nick prompted, and began to apply traction, pulling the head of the humerus away from the body just far enough for Frankie to thumb it back into position with an audible snick.

'Got it!' she said with satisfaction as she straightened up. 'Now all we need to do is take a picture to confirm reduction and rule out any fractures.'

'Can you move your fingers, Joe?' Nick prompted, and they all smiled when he complied. 'Good. Now, you know as well as I do that you'll be in a sling for a few days but if you want to regain the mobility in the joint, don't forget to exercise it.'

'Always remembering that for the first three weeks you mustn't combine lateral rotation with abduction,' Frankie added.

'Dear Lord, preserve me,' Joe groaned, his Scots accent somehow more pronounced than usual. 'Am I going to have every one of you clucking around me?'

'Probably,' Frankie confirmed cheerfully. 'You're one of us, and we take care of our own.'

He muttered something unintelligible under his

breath as Vicky helped him to sit up. He tried to don his shirt unaided but had to admit defeat in the end.

Frankie heard a phone ring in the reception area outside the room and suddenly looked around for a clock.

'Goodness! I've got patients waiting,' she announced. 'Vicky, I'll leave Joe in your capable hands. I've got to run.'

She was partway down the corridor before she realised that Nick was following her. She felt strangely vulnerable, knowing that he might be watching her, and instinct had her wanting to turn and confront him. Common sense told her that it was just a coincidence that they were both travelling in the same direction and she lengthened her stride.

'It won't work,' he said softly, easily keeping pace with her. 'My legs are longer than yours.'

She knew they were longer, and more muscled and patterned with intriguing dark hair that abraded her own legs when they…

'Avoidance isn't going to work,' he said bluntly, echoing her own despairing thoughts as they crossed the central atrium on their way to the GP unit.

'You might want to pretend that the connection between us doesn't exist,' he continued, his voice still forceful for all that he was keeping it low enough to reach only her ears. 'And you might want to cut me out of your life, but you can't do either of them. There *is* a connection, and unless either one of us leaves Edenthwaite, we're going to remain a part of each other's lives.'

There wasn't time for Frankie to reply, even if she could think of anything to say, as there was a waiting room full of patients waiting to be seen. In addition, she realised, the rest of the GPs on duty were going to have to share Joe's patients between them.

'Ladies and gentlemen,' Nick began, obviously having come to the same conclusion, 'Dr Faraday will be unable to see any patients today. Those of you who are waiting to see him are welcome to make another appointment if you'd rather not see another doctor. Those of you who need to be seen today, if you don't mind waiting, we'll share you out among us.'

'Shall I give the same message to people as they arrive?' Mara murmured to Frankie under cover of the ensuing hubbub of conversation.

'It might be worthwhile to phone the ones who haven't set off from home yet. It would save them a journey if they'd rather wait till Joe's back.'

'Can you tell me why he hasn't come in?' Mara probed delicately, aware of the many surrounding pairs of ears.

'Had a minor accident on his way to work,' Frankie said briefly, knowing that Mara was discreet enough to choose the right moment to pass the information on to the rest of the unit's staff. 'Could you give me a moment to get myself organised then send the first one in?'

It was such a pig of a day that Frankie was afraid she wasn't going to finish in time to collect Laura and Katie from school. That would have been the final irony, to have had to ask Nick to fetch them the very day after she'd told him it mustn't happen any more.

Laura was in such a bad mood, knowing that the disco was due to start in a matter of hours, that for the first time since the divorce Frankie actually breathed a sigh of relief when Martin's car receded down the lane taking the children away.

Then guilt swept over her. What sort of mother was she, to be relieved that her children were going away for a weekend?'

'A *normal* one,' she declared aloud, needing the affirmation of actually hearing the words. 'I'm not *just* a mother. That's only *one* facet of who I am.'

She gave a single nod for emphasis and set off for the kitchen, already planning what she was going to cook for her evening meal. Something…something that she didn't normally have because the children didn't like it. Something with ginger and spices and lots of crunchy vegetables. Definitely a stir-fried something.

Frankie stood in front of the cupboards, all the doors open while she took an assortment of herbs and spices out and added them to the growing selection.

When she finally served it out, her meal was the most glorious mixture of textures and flavours. The dish might never have made its way into the pages of any cookery book, but it was exactly what she needed tonight.

Decadent and self-indulgent.

And when she'd finished eating she was going to fall into bed with that romance novel she'd been meaning to read for weeks, and when she finally went to sleep it would be in the knowledge that she didn't have to get up until eight.

She was up at seven, hanging over the toilet being violently sick.

'Too many spices,' she groaned when she finally recovered enough to rinse her mouth out. 'Either that or the flu's finally got me.'

She crept out to the kitchen to put the kettle on, wondering if her stomach would let her have the cup of tea she wanted. Perhaps if she had a piece of toast it would settle down, the way it used to when she was pregnant with the girls.

If it didn't, she was going to have to phone the practice at eight to leave a message to find someone to cover for her.

She sighed wearily. This was the first time in a while that she'd managed to get her weekend shifts sorted out just right with plenty of work to fill the lonely hours until the girls came back. It would be just her luck to spend the time ill and to have to make up the duty when the girls were with her.

In the event, she was feeling a bit better by eight, and half an hour later was parking her car in a staff slot outside Denison Memorial ready to see whoever turned up for morning surgery.

Several times she heard Nick's voice in the corridor outside her consulting room and once, when she'd been called along to do some suturing to a young girl's face after a fall from her pony, she heard him organising an X-ray of a patient who'd come off his motorbike.

Each time she tried to ignore the fact that her pulse rate doubled, but it was impossible.

What was it about the man that just the sound of his voice was enough to make her hands tremble? How on earth was she going to manage to live and work in Edenthwaite without going completely mad? It didn't seem very likely that he was going to be moving any time soon. Vicky had returned to her roots here, and he seemed to be more than willing to put his roots down, too.

She hoped that uprooting herself and her daughters wasn't the only solution because she really didn't want to leave.

Anyway, where would she go?

Laura and Katie could hardly remember living any-
where else and had developed a wide circle of friends.
They would be completely lost if they had to move to
another school in another area.

Oh, Frankie knew it wasn't impossible. The families
of members of the armed forces could move as many
as seven times in as many years and *they* seemed to
survive.

But why put her girls through that if it wasn't necessary? All she had to do was develop a little self-
control.

'Yeah. That's all,' she scoffed when she found herself looking to see if Nick's four-by-four was still in
the car park.

'Get a life!' she exclaimed as she slammed the door
of her car and put the key in the ignition, suddenly
realising just how apt her children's catchphrase was.

Perhaps that was her problem. She'd spent so many
years living her life around the needs of her children
and her patients that she'd forgotten to fulfil her own
needs.

'So, what am I going to do about it?' she demanded,
then had to smile at the nonplussed motorist beside her
at the traffic lights who seemed to think that she was
talking to him.

'Perhaps I need a hobby,' she mused on her way to
examine a suspicious rash on a toddler who had just
started play school. What were the chances that there
was something infectious just about to sweep through
the community? Chickenpox, maybe?

'What about taking up a sport?' she continued to
herself. 'Or maybe joining some sort of group?
Amateur dramatics? Writing circle? Embroidery?'

She laughed derisively.

'Why not do all of them? After all, you've got so much spare time on your hands.' She concentrated on her driving for a moment, negotiating one of the cattle grids that separated the open moorland from the rest of the area.

'Let's face it, Frankie,' she said on a sudden chuckle that had more than a hint of hysteria. 'What you really need is a wife so that you'll have time to take up some of these things. A round of golf with Norman and his cronies, maybe.'

Or a husband, her subconscious said in a sly voice. Someone like Nick. Willing to collect children from school. Good at participating in family outings. Great at helping them with their homework. And if he happened to be the best lover in the world...

'The trouble is, I think there's only one Nick, and he's already spoken for,' she said in a sad voice, knowing she'd just come full circle.

Depression meant she didn't sleep much that night, most of it spent curled up in the corner of the settee with another in a seemingly endless stream of cups of tea. Even the book she'd been enjoying so much couldn't hold her attention and it was almost a relief when Sunday arrived and she could go back to Denison Memorial on the pretence that she had paperwork to do.

After her relief at seeing the girls leave so that she could have some peaceful time to herself, now she couldn't wait for them to return to bring some life back to the house.

Except, when they did return, they were both more subdued than ever, quiet enough for Frankie to worry if they were sickening for something.

Neither of them felt as if their temperatures were raised and each said that they felt all right, but she'd never seen them like this. It wasn't quite distress but it was definitely close to misery, and the most frustrating thing was that neither of them would talk to her.

'Perhaps you're just tired,' she suggested, normally the signal for both of them to perk up instantly.

'Maybe,' Laura agreed listlessly, and Frankie *knew* that there was something wrong. The thing she didn't know was how to find out what it was.

'Give it twenty-four hours,' she told herself as she came back down after seeing them to bed. 'Either they'll have bounced back from whatever it is, or it'll be time to ask some hard questions: If there's a problem, I need to know if there's something I can do to solve it.'

Monday morning started early...too early.

The alarm hadn't even rung but Frankie was already up...or rather down, on her knees in the bathroom in front of the toilet.

By the time she stopped being sick she didn't know whether she wanted to laugh or cry.

It was impossible.

She'd spent nearly two years sleeping with Martin without anything happening. She'd spent two nights with Nick and must have become instantly fertile because she was as sure as she could be without taking a test that she was pregnant.

She rinsed her mouth and sagged weakly onto the lid of the toilet, her head propped in her hands.

What on earth was she going to do?

She'd counselled any number of women over the years, from naïve underage teenagers to menopausal divorcees, enumerating their choices and advising them to try to balance their own situation with the needs of the new life they were carrying.

Some had opted for abortion, but she already knew that it was something she couldn't do. It might be the worst possible time for a pregnancy, with all the stresses of her non-relationship with Nick and Martin's threat to take the children. But she'd always longed to have another child, and to have one that had been fathered by Nick, the man she'd fallen in love with but could never have, was an almost miraculous bonus.

Not that *he* would see it that way, she realised soberly. From what she'd learned of him since he'd joined the staff at Denison Memorial, he was basically a very moral man with a well-developed sense of responsibility. If he knew she was expecting his child he would probably call off his marriage to Vicky.

She sighed heavily, knowing that she was going to have to find some way of hiding her condition until the two of them were married.

He wouldn't be happy, once he realised what she'd done, but it was the only answer. After the twelve years it had taken them to get together, he and Vicky deserved each other. She couldn't risk ruining everything for them.

Damn, this mountain of guilt was going to grow so big that it finally crushed her.

'Mum? Are you all right?' Laura demanded, looking impossibly young and innocent standing in the bathroom doorway with her hair all sleep-tangled around her worried face. 'I heard you being sick.'

For a moment Frankie's mind was paralysed, unable to come up with a single intelligible word.

'Ah, just one of the perils of being a doctor,' she

improvised after several dreadful seconds of blankness. 'I must have caught something from someone.'

Yeah, caught a pregnancy, the mocking voice inside her head quipped. How are you going to explain this after your mother-daughter talk about the birds and the bees and safe sex?

Frankie winced. She didn't want to think about that, not when she hadn't got used to the idea herself. Anyway, she needed to do a test first to make sure of the diagnosis.

'I'll be all right, sweetheart,' she said, hoping she sounded reassuring as she forced herself to concentrate on the normal everyday Monday morning routines. 'Has the alarm gone off yet? Do you want first go in the bathroom?'

Surely Laura's gaze was far too watchful for an eleven-year-old. Frankie almost found herself cringing as if *she* were the child.

'You're sure you're all right?' her daughter asked, and suddenly she was an uncertain girl again.

'Everything's going to be fine, sweetheart. I promise,' Frankie said, and held an arm out.

Like a shot Laura was burrowing against her side, almost as though she were only five again, and all the upset over the disco seemed to have vanished.

'I love you, Mum,' she muttered, and Frankie's heart swelled inside her.

'I love you, too, Laura,' she said, and tilted the precious face up towards her own before she added, 'I love you more than I can tell you. Even if you sulk and slam doors, I still love you. I might not *like* you very much...'

'But you still *love* me,' Laura finished, completing their family saying with a chuckle. Then she cocked a sly eyebrow. 'Enough to make porridge with sugar *and* cream again?'

By the time all three of them met at the table for breakfast it was almost as though the last few angst-ridden days had never happened.

Almost.

There was still a shadow behind the smile Laura threw her when she saw the swirl of cream decorating her bowl of porridge, but now that they were talking again Frankie was sure she would confide eventually.

Katie was back to her old self, bouncing with enthusiasm over the fact that she would be taking her next swimming test this afternoon.

Topics covered during the meal ranged from a query about whether Katie had remembered to put her costume and towel in her bag to a reminder that they needed to collect their books together for a trip to the library.

What Frankie could never have predicted was that Laura would look up from her empty bowl to ask, 'Mum, what's a vasectomy?'

CHAPTER NINE

SEVERAL hours later, Frankie still couldn't believe that they'd had that conversation.

There hadn't really been any way to duck it, not with Katie still finishing her breakfast and Laura looking as if she was going to sit there until she got an answer.

'It's a permanent method of contraception,' she'd said eventually, wondering what on earth had prompted the question in the first place and hoping that her explanation would be enough.

She should have known it wouldn't. That was one of the curses of having intelligent children who'd been brought up with the idea that if they didn't ask, they wouldn't learn.

'I know about contraception,' Katie piped up smugly. 'That's condoms and things for when you do sex and don't want to have a baby. I read about it in one of the magazines.'

'But vasectomy is different?' Laura probed. 'How?'

'Because it involves an operation to cut or tie the man's tubes so the seminal fluid can't get past any more,' Frankie detailed simply. 'He should only have it done if he doesn't want to have any more children because it's a very difficult operation to undo.'

'So he wouldn't be able to plant any more seeds to grow babies,' Katie added, reverting to the terminology she was more comfortable with.

'Exactly,' Frankie confirmed, still mystified that the topic had come up at all. 'Where did you hear about

it? Health education classes at school?' She'd been under the impression that the curriculum wouldn't be going into it that deeply until they reached senior school.

Katie began to speak, only to be silenced by Laura,
and Frankie almost missed the swift glare Laura had
directed at her younger sister.

'It's just something I heard and wondered what it
meant,' Laura said blandly, but some motherly instinct
told Frankie there was more to it than that.

Unfortunately, time was marching on and there
wasn't time to explore it now if they were going to get
to school and work.

Yet another topic to delve into at a later date, she
reminded herself with a silent groan as she chivvied
them out of the door.

Now she had a full morning of patients and because
she hadn't dared to eat anything more than a small
square of toast at breakfast for fear of being sick in
front of the girls, she was now starving.

'Coffee?' Jack offered when she stuck her head
around the door just long enough to grab the post from
her pigeonhole.

Frankie would have loved to have said yes but she
remembered only too well the effect the smell of coffee
had on the equilibrium of her stomach in the first few
weeks of a pregnancy.

'I think I'll just dunk a teabag and grab some biscuits,' she said, suiting her actions to her words while
concentrating on breathing as shallowly as possible
near his steaming mug.

She was just about to make her escape when he
called her back.

'Frankie, have you seen much of Nick recently?' he

asked, his usually cheerful face almost as overcast as the weather.

'Well, around the practice,' she hedged uncomfortably. 'I heard his voice when I was in on Saturday but other than that, not since he collected the girls the last time, I think.'

'What about Vicky? Have you seen her?'

'Not since she lent a hand when Joe dislocated his shoulder.' She frowned. 'Jack, what's this about? Have the two of them eloped or something?' Her stomach clenched at the thought and it had nothing to do with morning sickness.

'Chance would be a fine thing,' Jack muttered, and her curiosity was piqued enough to bring her back into the room in spite of the waft of coffee.

'Is there a problem?' she asked, feeling almost guilty to be inviting his confidence. Hopefully he would never know that she had a personal interest in Nick's relationship with Vicky.

'I don't know whether there's a problem or not,' he admitted, clearly puzzled. 'When they got engaged, Vicky was floating so high that I needed to tie a rope round her ankle to pull her back down to earth and she was spending all her spare time making lists and rushing around making arrangements for the wedding.'

'And?' She perched on the arm of a chair and began to nibble absently on a biscuit.

'And nothing,' he said with a shrug. 'Suddenly everything's gone quiet. I haven't even been told the date of the wedding—have you?'

'Sorry, not a word,' she confirmed, fighting to subdue the unreasonable bubble of hope that insisted on trying to surface.

Were the two of them having second thoughts? It

hardly seemed likely, not when it had taken them twelve years to progress to this point. There had only been that one brief conversation about breaking his engagement and she was almost certain that idea had been the result of Nick's fear that she might be pregnant. He certainly hadn't said any more about it to her.

'Well, if you hear anything...'

Frankie made commiserating noises then set off on her thoughtful way towards her consulting room, only to walk straight into the woman in question. It was almost as if she'd been surreptitiously lying in wait to catch her.

'Frankie, could I have a word? Have you got a minute?' Vicky asked, clearly uncomfortable.

As ever, Frankie couldn't help feeling guilty in her presence but the younger woman looked so nervous that she needed to do something to lighten the atmosphere.

'As long as you don't mind if I finish my breakfast,' she joked, holding up the handful of biscuits. 'One of the penalties of being a full-time working mother.'

She led the way into the room and dumped the armful of paperwork on the desk before she sat in one of the chairs in front of it, gesturing to Vicky to take the other to strike a less formal setting.

'How can I help?' she offered, and took another bite, careful not to drop crumbs on the clean floor.

'I don't know if you can,' Vicky muttered, but perched on the edge of the chair anyway. 'It's just... Well, I hope you won't take this the wrong way, but you're a bit of an outsider in Edenthwaite so you wouldn't have the same sort of axe to grind as some of the others. *And* you're a woman.'

Frankie thought it was best to let her ramble her way

to the point. She was obviously troubled about something and pushing might make her clam up.

'I know you're about ten years older than I am,' she began again, and Frankie had to keep her indignant correction to eight years inside her head. 'But do you think it makes a relationship more difficult when there's more than a couple of years' difference in age between a couple?'

There was only six years between Nick and Vicky, a fact she must have known for the last twelve years. Why was she suddenly worrying about it now?

'It depends on the individuals involved,' she replied carefully. 'Some people are very mature for their age and others are very young. Personally, I would be wary of anything more than a generation because of the relative life expectancy of the partners.'

'You mean the older one is likely to die earlier.'

'Statistically,' Frankie agreed. 'But that's not to say that you don't get some people dying in their thirties and others going on past their century, so if you pick someone with the right genes… Anyway, there's only six years between you and Nick, so it doesn't really apply, does it.'

The mention of Nick's name seemed to flick a switch somewhere in Vicky's head that brought her back from her internal thoughts.

'Of course not,' she agreed absently, then focused, her cheeks colouring slightly. 'Actually, I was also wondering it you could give me a once-over and a prescription for the Pill.'

Frankie flicked a quick glance at the clock and saw that she still had time before her first patient was due.

'No problem,' she said, standing up to get her stethoscope and sphygmomanometer. 'I take it you want a repeat prescription for whatever you're taking at the moment?'

'No. Um. Actually, I've never taken anything before because I haven't needed to,' she admitted with an unexpected touch of shyness for a qualified nurse.

It was rather more than Frankie needed to know about the woman Nick was going to marry. It implied that she had actually loved him enough for the last twelve years to wait for him to be her first lover. Frankie couldn't help but admire her steadfastness.

At the same time she was struck by the uncomfortable thought that lack of any sexual activity with his fiancée might have been one of the reasons why Nick had been so keen to sleep with *her*.

That was something else she was going to have to think about later.

'Well, if you're intending to wait a while before starting your family it would be a good idea to start taking it straight away to make sure the brand agrees with you. We can always change it for another if it doesn't. Anyway, you need a month to get the drug into your system before you're officially "safe" from pregnancy.'

While she carried out the routine checks and asked the usual questions to ascertain Vicky's suitability to take the Pill, she couldn't help pondering on the strange irony of the situation.

Here she was, the woman pregnant with Nick's baby, giving advice on how to avoid pregnancy to his future wife.

'By the way,' she called just as Vicky was about to leave the room with her prescription in her hand. 'You wouldn't happen to have heard how Joe is doing, would you? Is he up to driving yet or do you think he needs someone to do some shopping for him?'

'He's all right,' the younger woman said without turning back. 'I... Someone's already been up to check on him.'

'Good,' Frankie said, but she was speaking to herself.

The rest of the morning was fairly routine, but just as she thought her afternoon of home visits was going to allow her to be standing at the school gates ahead of time everything went wrong.

She'd arrived to check on one of her older patients, newly returned home just three weeks post-operative after a much-needed hip replacement, to find her lying on the floor in agony.

'Miss Phipps, what *have* you done to yourself?' Frankie said as she hurried towards the little bird-like creature huddled on the stone floor. It was a good job they'd arranged a secret place to leave a key or she might have had to find a way to break in when the fiercely independent retired schoolteacher didn't answer the door.

'I dropped an egg and slipped on the mess,' she said in disgust. 'At least I didn't fall on my new hip.'

'Unfortunately, I think you've broken the other one,' Frankie had to tell her. 'I'm going to have to phone for an ambulance and get you to hospital.'

She pressed the speed dial function on the mobile that would connect her directly to the switchboard at Denison Memorial and within moments was able to confirm that a unit was on its way.

'You couldn't put the kettle on, could you?' Miss Phipps asked weakly. 'That was almost the worst part about lying here so long. I've been so thirsty.'

'I'm so sorry, but it would be better if I didn't give you anything until we find out what's wrong. If you need to go into Theatre, we don't want to have to wait for hours until your stomach's had time to empty.'

'I suppose you're right,' she sighed. 'In that case, can I get you to put some things into a bag for me? The gowns in the hospital are so enormous it's like trying to live in a tent. And as for the necklines... Well!'

Frankie had to chuckle. She could just imagine what the elderly spinster thought about the way the neck of the hospital-issue gowns would slip revealingly off her narrow shoulders.

By the time she'd supervised her patient's departure and locked up her little cottage, she knew she was going to be pushed to arrive at the school in time. The bell should be ringing in about five minutes and her journey would take at least fifteen. Thank goodness the staff knew that delays were sometimes unavoidable and they were willing to wait with the children until they were collected. There was a sense of security in knowing that they were prepared for such eventualities.

Except, when she pulled up outside the school the doors were already closed and all the lights were turned off except for one that might have been the principal's office.

'I can just imagine what Laura will say if she's had to wait in Mrs Harrison's office,' Frankie muttered as she crossed the playground. That was apparently one of the punishments for children who misbehaved—to have to do their work under the head teacher's eagle eye.

All was quiet as she made her way along the corridor

and as she knocked on the door she was musing that schools all seemed to have the same smell about them.

'Hello, Dr Long. What can I do for you?' Mrs Harrison asked pleasantly, beckoning her into the brightness of her sanctuary.

'Oh, I've only come to collect Laura and Katie,' Frankie said. 'Unfortunately I was delayed getting a patient transferred to hospital so I'm a bit late.'

'Collect Laura and Katie?' the head teacher repeated with a sudden frown. 'But they were collected some time ago. There are no children left on the premises.'

'Collected? Who collected them? When?' Suddenly Frankie was immersed in a parent's worst nightmare. 'I didn't ask anyone to come for them because I knew I was only going to be a few minutes late.'

'Oh, my…' Mrs Harrison whirled and strode across to consult a brightly coloured chart on the wall then reached for the phone on her desk. 'I'm phoning the member of staff who was on playground duty this afternoon. He will know who collected— Anthony? Helen here. I need to know who collected Laura and Katie Long this afternoon.'

Frankie waited with bated breath, unaccountably relieved when Mrs Harrison smiled and said her good-byes.

'Panic over,' she said happily. 'They were collected by their father.'

'Their *father*?' Frankie repeated in disbelief. 'Are you sure? Martin *never* collects them from school. He doesn't finish work till after five.'

'I'm quite sure. Mr Clitheroe asked for identification but he said it wasn't really necessary when the girls were calling him Daddy.'

Still stunned by what had happened, Frankie barely remembered her manners before she left the school.

What on earth was Martin doing in Edenthwaite at this time of the afternoon and why had he decided to collect the girls? He'd never done it before.

She was already halfway home when she realised that this might have something to do with his decision to ask for the children to come to live with him. Had this been some sort of spying mission so that he could gather evidence that she was a neglectful mother?

It was so much worse than that, Frankie learned when she found the letter waiting for her on the kitchen table.

Not only had Martin collected the girls from school but he'd also brought them home to collect their belongings before driving them to his house.

'In view of the immoral nature of your behaviour I have had no option but to remove my daughters from your sphere of influence,' his pompous letter stated with relish, and she collapsed in a heap on the kitchen floor as all the strength left her legs.

The only person Frankie could think to contact was Nick.

If her brain had been working more rationally she would probably have realised that it was inappropriate to involve him when it was her behaviour with him that had brought this disaster about. Although how anyone had found out about what had happened between them was another matter entirely.

As it was, her hand had reached automatically for the phone and the only number she could remember was his.

'Nick, I need you,' she blurted when he answered,

too panic-struck to monitor her words, her teeth beginning to chatter as shock set in. 'M-Martin has taken the girls away. He—he took them from school. He—he left a l-letter—'

'Shh, Frankie. I'm on my way,' he broke in when she couldn't get the words out fast enough because her brain seemed to be paralysed. 'Put the kettle on. I'll be there by the time you've made the tea.'

He broke the connection with a decisive click but it was several seconds before she could bring herself to break even that tenuous connection with him.

True to his word, she heard him drawing up behind her car as she poured the freshly brewed tea into two mugs.

He didn't need to knock on the door. By the time he reached it she'd already pulled it open and was waiting for him with tears rolling down her face.

'Ah, Frankie, don't,' he crooned as he took her in his arms and wrapped her up tight against his body. 'We'll sort it out. I promise we'll sort it all out.'

'B-but how?' she wailed against his shoulder. 'He's a lawyer and his letter says—'

'Lawyers still have to put their trousers on one leg at a time, the same as the rest of the world,' he pointed out rudely, but the silly image was enough to grant her a measure of control. 'Now, Frankie, can you show me this letter?'

It didn't take him long to scan it but his face remained so expressionless that she had no idea what he was thinking about it. Was he blaming himself for his part in her troubles? Perhaps he—

'Was there any official documentation with this?' he demanded suddenly, gripping each of her shoulders in his hands.

She shook her head. 'Nothing. That's the envelope and that's all there was in it.'

'Right. Good. I need to use your phone a minute,' he said rather distractedly as he searched through his wallet for something. Whatever it was, he seemed to have found it when he drew out what looked like a business card.

'Simon?' he said when the phone was answered at the other end. 'Nick Johnson here. I need a bit of urgent advice.'

It was a good job he was using a cordless phone because over the next few minutes Nick marched several miles up and down the room as he explained the situation. Frankie was sitting cringing at the thought that he was going to say something about the intimacy between the two of them, but it was never mentioned.

Finally the connection was broken and Nick turned to face her.

'He's working on it,' he said seriously, as if Frankie should know what he was talking about.

'Working on what? Getting the girls back?' She didn't let herself dare to hope. Martin was a lawyer who knew his business inside out, and his speciality was family law.

'I'm sorry, Frankie. I should have explained.' He came to sit beside her and took her hands in his, rubbing them gently when he felt how cold they were. 'That was Simon, an old family friend who just happens to be rather prominent in the field of family law. Since his wife tried to disappear with their children he's developed a particular interest in custody arrangements and at this very moment is checking to see what he can do for you.'

'Does he think he can?'

'He's too wily to say anything before he's done some checking, but it sounds as if Martin has rather jumped the gun.'

'Jumped the gun? How?'

'By taking the children away from the custodial home before he'd formalised any change in the arrangements. He's made an unsubstantiated accusation to use as an excuse, but as a lawyer he should have known that it wasn't enough.'

'He was probably counting on the fact that I wouldn't know any better.'

'He'd forgotten the old saying, "It's not *what* you know but *who* you know that counts." Simon is going to do some phoning and then he'll get back to us with the results. It might not be until the morning, depending who's left work early on a Monday, but—'

He was interrupted by the phone and reached across to snatch it up.

'Hello? Simon! That was quick. What news?' Nick listened for several minutes with a serious expression that didn't betray a single emotion. Frankie was just getting ready to scream with frustration when he turned to her with a smile. 'Do you think the other members of the practice could do without you tomorrow morning? Simon's got you an appointment in court at nine.'

'What about Martin and the girls? Will they be there?' Her heart was pounding so fast that her whole body was shaking. She hated the feeling that her life was out of control and at the moment it felt as if it had exploded into a million fragments.

'He'll be ringing Martin as soon as he finishes talking to us. Now, can you make it tomorrow morning?'

'Of course I can, Nick. On my hands and knees if

necessary. We're talking about Laura and Katie and the fact that Martin's trying to take them away from me.'

He turned back to the phone. 'That's a yes, Simon. See you there at about eight-thirty.'

He returned to sit beside her and pulled her close but Frankie found it hard to respond for a moment. Everything had happened so fast that her head was spinning.

'You said that you'd see him at eight-thirty?' she said, picking up on his last words.

'Actually, *we*'ll be seeing him at eight-thirty so he can ask you some questions before you go into court. I thought you'd like some moral support.'

'Oh Nick…' she began, her voice rising to a wail as the enormity of the situation started to dawn on her. She shouldn't impose on him. She had no right. Oh, but it made such a difference having him here with her, especially when she could bury her face in the solid curve of his shoulder.

'Oh, Nick, I'm so afraid I'm going to lose my babies. What will I do if Martin won't give them back? He wasn't even interested in them till he got married again.'

'That's one of the things we're going to tell Simon tomorrow morning.'

'But what good can he do?' she cried, noticing that he'd said *we* but at the moment unable to take much comfort from it. 'It's all there in Martin's letter.'

'All we know at the moment are the grounds he's going to use to try to take the girls away, but he has to prove them, which he hasn't, and he has to go through all the proper channels, which he hasn't.'

Nick paused to hook a gentle finger under her chin, lifting until she was looking up into his caring blue eyes. 'At the moment, he's gone against the custody agreement without your knowledge or consent. Apparently he could actually be accused of kidnapping Laura and Katie and that wouldn't look good on his CV.'

'But—'

'Look, Frankie, I don't pretend to know anything much about the law, but I do trust Simon and I know he's probably got more contacts within the profession than any lawyer has a right to. That's because he's one in a very long line of brilliant lawyers, barristers and judges who all command the utmost respect from their colleagues. If there's anything that *can* be done, you can be certain that Simon will do it.'

The phone rang again and Nick reached out for it as easily as if it were his own house.

'Hello?'

Frankie recognised the voice on the other end, demanding to know who was speaking. She cringed, but when she held out her hand for the phone Nick ignored her.

'Who is this?' he demanded briskly.

'Martin Long. I'm Frankie's husband and I want to have a word with her,' she heard him say belligerently, and noticed that he seemed to have forgotten that he was now her *ex*-husband. 'Anyway, who are you? One of the men she entertains at all times of the day and night?'

'My name is Dr Johnson and I work at Denison Memorial,' Nick said with icy precision. 'I am treating Dr Long for shock because someone has kidnapped her daughters.'

'Kidnapped?' Frankie cringed when she saw Nick wince at the volume of the shout. 'Does the bloody woman know what that sort of accusation could do to my career? And how the hell did she get hold of someone like Simon—'

Nick had obviously had enough of his ranting.

'Sorry to butt in, but at the moment Dr Long is waiting for her legal counsel to get back to her so she'd rather you didn't tie the line up. I look forward to meeting you tomorrow morning.'

He broke the connection with a deliberate click before turning to her with a wicked grin. 'I think we've got him rattled.' He chortled and wrapped both arms around her for a hug that felt deliciously like coming home.

'Thank you, Nick,' she said fervently. 'It seems such a small thing to say when you've done so much for me but—'

'No thanks necessary,' he said softly. 'At least not until Laura and Katie are back home again to stay. Then we'll have to have a celebration.'

'A celebration and a half,' she corrected with a watery smile. 'I promise. But there's still tomorrow morning to get through.'

'Well, how do you want to spend the night, then? Watching your favourite videos? Watching your least favourite videos? Listening to music? Seducing me and ravishing my poor puny body all night?'

Frankie had been torn between welcoming his company through the fraught hours and telling him that he should go home but the wicked expression on his face when he'd tacked on that last suggestion destroyed any resistance with a burst of laughter.

Nick gazed down at the woman who'd finally fallen asleep in his arms and smiled wryly.

She'd obviously thought he was joking about the seduction and had settled for a diet of slightly fuzzy videos played on a machine that was obviously in dire need of servicing. Just one of those little jobs that she didn't have the time to notice, let alone do anything about. The sort of thing he'd be able to do for her if only…

He sighed deeply and pondered for a moment on the vagaries of timing and coincidence. There were so many things that had brought him to this place with this woman, any one of which could have changed the course of his life.

If his sister hadn't suffered from a Wilms' tumour requiring chemotherapy and surgery he'd never have spent so much time in hospital, keeping her spirits up. Having decided on a career in medicine, it had been sheer chance that he and Jack had gained places at the same teaching hospital and become such close friends.

Had he never met Vicky, he would never have ended up coming to Denison Memorial, and if he hadn't decided to call in one day early he would never have been sent to Frankie's house.

And if he'd never got to know Frankie, he'd never have known what real soul-deep love felt like. The sort of love that moved mountains and changed the course of history.

The sort of love that he still had to find out if Frankie shared.

CHAPTER TEN

NICK sighed as he leant his head back in the corner of the settee. For the first time in years he was almost content in spite of the messy situation that surrounded him.

Hopefully, the custody matter would be resolved in a matter of hours, but the tangled relationship between Frankie and himself might take a little longer.

It had taken him enough time to realise what was going on. With his track record, taking things at face value wasn't an option.

Oh, he'd known that Frankie was someone special right from their first meeting, and that had been *before* the mind-blowing sex.

It had been long overdue, but yesterday he'd finally sat down with Vicky to talk everything through. If only he hadn't taken the easy way out when he'd met up with her again, how different the last month or two would have been for everyone…

He groaned aloud then froze when Frankie stirred, not wanting to wake her. She needed all the sleep she could get if she was going to cope with tomorrow.

But, having straightened everything out with Vicky, he needed to talk to Frankie—now. He needed to explain what had happened in the last twenty-four hours and that would mean going into all the things that had led up to them. He knew he didn't come out of the tale very well, but he wasn't going to settle for anything less than honesty.

This wasn't the right time, though. He was impatient, but he was going to have to wait until the custody question was settled.

It had taken him long enough to see what had been right in front of his nose. A few more hours would be frustrating but ultimately the only thing that mattered was that Frankie gave him the chance to explain.

The course of the rest of his life depended on it.

Frankie began the slow rise towards wakefulness with a mixture of feelings.

There was an impression of security and warmth wrapped around her that she really didn't want to leave, but there was also a hefty dose of apprehension and a feeling that there were dark shadows hovering just beyond her view.

'Frankie,' crooned a husky voice somewhere nearby, and she smiled lazily. Her imagination had come up with a pretty good impression of Nick's voice. Good enough for her to be able to remember the scent of his skin and the hint of laundry soap in his shirt.

'Frankie, love. It's time to wake up,' the voice murmured, more insistently this time, and she finally realised that it wasn't all a figment of her imagination.

'Nick?' She opened her eyes just a tiny bit and found herself looking into the deep blue of his at extremely close quarters. 'What are you doing h—? Oh!' The memories of yesterday's events returned with a crash.

'Time to get ready,' he said quietly, the way he tightened his arms around her showing that he understood only too well the reason why her eyes had instantly filled with tears. 'I let you sleep as long as possible, but if we're going to get there in time for the meeting…'

The meeting. Panic had her trying to sit up but Nick didn't immediately open his arms to release her.

'There's just one thing before you go,' he said quickly, then bent his head to press a gentle kiss to her mouth. 'That's for luck.'

Speechless, Frankie gazed into his caring blue eyes and wondered what she'd done to deserve this man in her life. He wasn't hers to keep, but without his presence she certainly wouldn't be coping with today's events. In fact, without him she would probably be facing losing her daughters to her ex-husband's machinations. She certainly wouldn't have known who to go to for help, let alone at such short notice.

'Nick… I might not have said it as often as I should, but you'll probably never know just how grateful I've been for your…for your friendship and help since you came to Edenthwaite.'

'You're not going sloppy on me, are you, Dr Long?' he teased, and shifted just far enough so that she could get her feet on the floor. 'There isn't time for that now. We'll have to talk about it after we collect Laura and Katie. Now, do you need any help in the shower?'

Those eyebrows were going up and down again like a bad impression of Groucho Marx while he pretended to leer at her.

'Idiot!' She giggled and set off towards the bathroom.

'*Lovable* idiot?' he called after her, and she silently agreed with his alteration. He was a very lovable man. A man she would probably love the rest of her life, especially with his child to remind her of their time together.

That was another thing they were going to have to talk about *when* they finally found the time to start on the growing list of subjects. Not now, with his wedding approaching, but one day soon because he did have a right to know that he'd fathered her baby. How she was going to tell Laura and Katie was another matter entirely.

By eight-thirty terror was making her feel worse than morning sickness.

For some unknown reason, that form of nausea hadn't struck this morning so she hadn't been left with difficult explanations to make to Nick. As it was, her stomach was tied in knots at the prospect that if she gave a wrong answer, she could lose her daughters for all but alternate weekends and a share of school holidays. How would she know what was a wrong answer if she didn't know what a right one was?

Simon was calm and very professional and had tried his best to reassure her but by the time they went into the chambers where the meeting was to be held, the only thing keeping her from hysteria was Nick's hand holding hers tightly.

After one quick glance around the beautiful old oak-panelled walls the only thing she was interested in seeing was her precious girls.

'Laura,' she croaked as tears welled in her eyes. 'Katie.'

'Mum!' Katie called, and pulled her hand out of her father's grasp to run to her.

Such a precious little body, Frankie thought as she crouched down to hug her tightly, completely uncaring of the fact that she might crease her carefully chosen suit.

'Don't cry, Mum,' Katie pleaded, her own eyes rapidly filling with tears. 'We're sorry we didn't tell you where we were going but Dad said he'd let you know.'

Laura stood silently watching them. Frankie could see some unknown conflict clear on her daughter's face. Her slender shoulders were stiff with hard-won control but there was nothing she could do about the silvery tracks of misery on her cheeks and Frankie's heart went out to her. This was the thing she'd dreaded—that the children would end up playing piggy-in-the-middle between their parents.

'Come and take a seat, Dr Long. Make yourself comfortable,' invited the elderly gentleman ensconced in a comfortable wing chair with all the presence of a king on his throne. 'I prefer to settle such matters in more informal surroundings for the sake of the children involved.'

'Thank you,' she murmured shakily, needing Nick's help when her trembling legs wouldn't let her straighten up. She glanced across at Martin and, as she'd expected, found him glaring daggers at her.

Frankie knew that every word of this meeting was vital but for several minutes the preliminaries went straight over her head.

All she could see was the increasingly overweight, definitely pompous figure of the man she'd once loved enough to marry. All she could think was that she really hadn't known him at all and she didn't think he could really have loved her if he could do something like this to her.

'So it's in the best interests of the children for the custody arrangements to be reversed,' Martin was saying. 'Not only will they be taken away from undesirable influences but they'll be part of a two-parent family again, with a mother willing to stay home to devote herself to them full time.'

In spite of the fact that she was feeling increasingly sick, Frankie had to admit that in full oratorical flow Martin could be quite impressive. Unfortunately, the person he most had to make an impact on looked less than pleased to be lectured at full volume.

Without comment, he turned to Simon and silently invited him to speak.

'Frankie is at a total loss,' he said simply. 'For the seven years since she divorced him for adultery, she has raised Laura and Katie to be loving, outgoing, confident children with very little input from their busy father. Suddenly, when he remarries, Mr Long decides to level unfounded accusations at his ex-wife in an attempt to have the custody agreement reversed, then compounds his perfidy by kidnapping them from school.'

Martin was nearly purple in the face and looked close to exploding with outrage by the time Simon finished.

'They are *not* unfounded,' he declared heatedly when he was permitted to speak. 'And I only took the girls home with me for their own well-being.'

Frankie had been growing more and more concerned about the effect it was having on the girls as the level of acrimony went up. She'd been watching the way they turned from one speaker to the other almost as if they were watching a tennis match, their expressions a mixture of worry and fear.

Suddenly, Laura burst into tears, sobbing loudly.

'Stop it, Daddy. Please!' she wailed. 'It's *my* fault. It's *all* my fault.'

'Laura, sweetheart…' Frankie was out of her chair

and across the room in a flash, sinking to her knees again to wrap comforting arms around her weeping daughter.

'I'm sorry, Mum. I didn't m-mean for all this to happen. But you w-wouldn't listen to what I w-wanted and—'

'Shh! Shh!' Frankie soothed, drawing the eleven-year-old onto her lap and rocking her as though she were still a toddler. 'Calm down and catch your breath, sweetheart. Everything's going to be all right.'

It took several minutes, the loan of Nick's handker-chief and a glass of water, but eventually the storm subsided.

'Now, young lady,' began the eminent man who had waited without a hint of impatience for the crisis to subside. 'I believe you can tell us something that will shed a bit of light on matters.'

Laura gulped and nodded wordlessly, shrinking back into the reassuring shelter of Frankie's arms.

'Supposing you tell me what's been happening.'

'Where shall I start?' she began in a hesitant voice, sounding far younger than her usual confident self.

'Wherever you like,' he invited. 'How about starting where it all began?'

Laura nodded again and thought for a minute.

'That would be when Dad got married again and 'Licia said she wanted to give us a baby brother or sister.'

Martin started to interrupt but a fierce glare under bushy white eyebrows had him subsiding.

'Oh, she didn't tell Katie and me. She was talking to Dad when we were there one weekend and Dad told her he couldn't have any children because he'd had a vasectomy when Katie was on the way.'

'What?' Frankie gasped, shocked into speech. 'You had a vasectomy? While I was pregnant?' She suddenly realised that she was speaking out of turn and put her hand over her mouth. 'I'm sorry, sir… Your Honour…' she mumbled with her cheeks on fire.

'Am I to take it that you never told your wife that you'd taken permanent measures against any further children?' he asked Martin, every word knife-edged in the sudden silence.

'Ah… Well…' Martin hesitated, his eyes darting around the room almost as if he was searching out an escape route. He certainly couldn't meet Frankie's eyes.

'Speak up, man!' he was ordered irritably, sharp grey eyes merciless.

'Well, no, I didn't,' Martin admitted.

'I see.' He didn't need to say any more for his feelings to be made obvious, then he turned back to Laura with an encouraging smile. 'I'm sorry about that interruption, young lady. Please, continue.'

'Well, then Dad told Katie and me that we were going to be living with him and 'Licia soon, because Mum didn't have time to look after us properly, but it's not true. She does look after us. She loves us. But she's a doctor and sometimes she has to work, but she always makes sure that we've got someone to stay with us when she's on call.'

She broke off from her narrative a moment.

'I don't know if you know what that means,' she said kindly. 'But sometimes it's her turn to go to the people who are ill in the night but she never leaves us alone.'

Frankie caught the gleam of humour in the elderly

man's eyes at the explanation, but he never betrayed it to Laura.

'Anyway,' she went on more soberly, 'there was going to be a disco at school and I really, really wanted to go but Mum wouldn't ask Dad if we could change the visitation weekend.' She hung her head a moment. 'I was so cross that I told Dad that Mum had men staying in our house at night.'

Martin wasn't the only one to make a sound but where his was a subdued crow of triumph, Frankie's was a moan of comprehension.

'So, *did* your mother have men staying in your house at night?' The bushy white eyebrows pulled together into a frown.

'Well, yes and no,' Laura admitted. 'When our usual babysitter got sick, Dr Jack came to sit with us when Mum had to go to the patients, but then a baby was coming and something had gone wrong so they needed Dr Jack to go and help with a Caesarean. That's when they have to cut the mother's stomach to get the baby out,' she added helpfully, before continuing her narrative. 'Dr Jack asked Nick to sit with us until Mum came home because he knows that Nick collects us from school sometimes.'

'I see.' The white head nodded sagely. 'Well, thank you for telling us, Laura. Is there anything else you want to add?'

'Not really, except…' She turned on Frankie's lap to look up at her. 'Except I'm really sorry, Mum. I was cross that I couldn't go to the disco. I shouldn't have told Dad those things but I didn't know that he was going to take us away. Katie and me don't want to go and live with him.'

'Is this true, young lady?' It was Katie's turn to be

in the spotlight but she didn't seem to be in the least bit intimidated.

'No. We'd rather live with Mum,' she said with a big happy smile. 'Especially if she's going to have more babies.'

There were several seconds of stunned silence before pandemonium erupted with everybody speaking at once.

'Katie! I told you not to tell,' Laura wailed as she leapt to her feet.

'Babies?' Nick and Martin echoed each other in varying degrees of shock, but where Martin glared at her in complete horror, Nick's face was wreathed in an inexplicable smile.

Simon didn't say a word but he sent Nick a telling look.

'Oh, Lord!' Frankie groaned and covered her face. She'd never dreamed that Laura would put two and two together so fast. How was she ever going to be able to face Vicky? And why on earth was Nick smiling? This was the *last* thing he needed to find out.

The sound of a throat being very loudly cleared finally broke through the hubbub.

'Well, people, if we could all be silent for a moment,' he suggested firmly enough for it to be an outright order. 'As far as I can see, there is absolutely no reason for any change to be made in the existing custody order.'

'But…' Martin began, but got no further, silenced by nothing more than a glare.

'In view of the nature of the misunderstanding and the fact that it has been so swiftly resolved,' the eminent man continued heavily, pinning Martin as effectively as a bug on a pin, 'there will be no kidnapping charge in spite of the fact that your actions were ill-advised and precipitate. Be advised that I would not easily tolerate any repetition.'

He turned to Frankie, still kneeling on the floor as she couldn't find an ounce of energy to get to her feet.

'As for you, young woman. Your devotion to your daughters is commendable and they are both a credit to you. It's almost a shame that you didn't have a few more,' he added in a musing tone, a definite twinkle in his eye.

Frankie didn't know whether to smile back or to wish for the floor to open up and swallow her. Nick's hand at her elbow, urging her to her feet, didn't help much in making the decision. She couldn't even bring herself to look at him, knowing that her guilty secret had come out like that.

'Mum, does that mean we can come home now?' Katie demanded in a stage whisper.

'Yes, young lady. That's exactly what it means,' he announced as he got up out of his chair and leant forward to offer his hand to each girl in turn. 'I'm very pleased to have met you,' he said. 'Make sure you take good care of your mother.'

'We will,' Laura said.

'Of course,' Katie agreed pertly, then leant forward to add in a hoarse whisper, '*And* the baby. Do you want to know what it is when it arrives?'

'I would love to know,' he whispered back with a smile, then straightened to continue. 'Now, off you people go and let me do some work.'

Martin was pale and tight-lipped as he led the way out of the chambers, not even glancing in their direction in his hurry to leave.

That didn't bother Frankie nearly as much as the

prospect of the next conversation she needed to have with Nick. So far he hadn't said a word to her but she knew that couldn't last.

She even contemplated keeping the girls home for the rest of the day but that would just have been delaying the inevitable.

The journey back towards Edenthwaite was strangely subdued. She'd expected both girls to have been full of recent events but even the normally ebullient Katie was sitting quietly in the back of Nick's four-by-four. Perhaps they were growing old enough to recognise the tension building up in the front of the vehicle.

Finally, just when she was beginning to think she couldn't stand it any more, Nick cleared his throat and broke the fraught silence.

'I've been waiting for the chance to tell you how much you all mean to me,' he began quietly, his deep voice travelling easily over the hushed efficiency of the powerful engine. 'I know I only met you a few weeks ago but in some ways it feels as if I've known you for years, and today...' He broke off to clear his throat again and Frankie realised that he had almost let his emotions get the better of him.

She glanced over her shoulder and found Laura and Katie completely spellbound by Nick's words, their eyes fixed on the rear-view mirror so that they could watch his face.

'Today,' he continued, 'I couldn't have been more proud of all of you if you had been my own family.'

'Nick?' Katie piped up tentatively. 'Does that mean you love us?'

'Yes, squirt,' he said with a rusty chuckle. 'It means that I love you.'

'Enough to marry us?' she added eagerly, but Frankie hastily broke in before he had a chance to answer. She shouldn't have him put on the spot like that. It just wasn't fair.

'Enough questions, Katie,' she declared. 'I think it would be a good idea if we looked for somewhere to have something to eat and then you can go straight to school when we get back to Edenthwaite.'

'Oh, Mu-u-m!' both girls exclaimed in disgust.

'Can't we go back tomorrow?' Laura pleaded. 'We want to ask Nick—'

'You'll have to go to school this afternoon because Nick and I won't be free to look after you. This isn't a holiday, you know,' she added sternly, and was grateful to find that she'd squashed any sign of rebellion.

She was glad they hadn't continued the argument because she'd actually stretched the truth somewhat. The phone call last night to Mark Fletcher, manager at Denison Memorial, to inform him of the hastily arranged meeting this morning, had actually been met with the instruction to take as long as they needed. He would monitor the situation in the GP unit to organise cover if necessary.

Frankie fully realised that it meant that once Laura and Katie had been delivered to their teachers, she and Nick would have the time to sit down and clear the air.

Her stomach clenched uneasily at the idea but there was no alternative. She couldn't live with guilty secrets weighing her down any more.

'Coffee?' Nick offered when Frankie sank uneasily onto one of the chairs at the kitchen table. 'Or are you one of those women who can't bear the smell even of decaffeinated when she's pregnant?'

With that question Frankie knew the gloves were off but, instead of apprehension, suddenly all she felt was relief that they were finally going to get things straightened out.

'Nick, I was going to tell you,' she began placatingly when she saw the tension in his jaw.

'When? Today? This week? Next?'

'Well, later,' she admitted with a return of the guilt that had plagued her for weeks. 'After you and Vicky—'

'Frankie, there *is* no me and Vicky any more, as of the night before last.'

'What! But the wedding—'

'Is off,' he finished firmly, sitting down on the chair at right angles to her. In that position he couldn't help but see every expression that crossed her face but he was also close enough to take possession of her hand. The fact that the contact between them completely scrambled her thought processes and made her pulse race wasn't something that had changed, guilty or not.

'So,' he began again, 'I think it's time to start putting our cards on the table, and as most of the guilt is mine, I'll go first.'

'But…' She subsided when he briefly pressed a silencing finger to her lips.

'I was engaged to marry a fellow doctor,' he announced suddenly, and shock robbed her of any desire to speak. 'I thought we were two of a kind until I discovered that she was being paid money under the counter to massage the data on some drugs trials we were doing. It was hard to shop her because I couldn't really believe that I'd misjudged her so badly, but if I hadn't, I wouldn't have been able to live with myself. Never mind the possibility that I might have been tarred with the same brush, the prospect of drugs being licensed for use based on falsified safety data was...' He shook his head.

'I decided to change direction and chose to train as a GP. When I met up with Vicky again, I suppose it was her transparent air of...of *innocence* that attracted me more than anything else. I'm not proud of it,' he admitted candidly. 'In fact, that's part of the guilt I've been hauling around for months. I knew when she was a kid that she'd had a massive crush on me and when I realised she still had feelings for me I knew she was someone who wouldn't cheat, wouldn't lie. It just didn't occur to me that she deserved something better than the affection I felt for her...until I met you.'

'But, Nick. She loves you,' Frankie insisted, empathising with the caring young woman she'd last seen taking care of Joe Faraday. 'You can't hurt her by cancelling the wedding.'

'You would rather our baby was born a bastard?' he challenged, but there was no heat in it.

'Of course not, but...' Frustrated that she couldn't find the words she needed when she wanted them, Frankie retrieved her hand to rake the fingers through her hair. 'I didn't do it on purpose, you know. Get pregnant, I mean.'

'I'd already worked that out, sweetheart, as soon as I heard about the vasectomy,' he said with a smile, capturing her hand again. 'But I'm not sorry.'

'You're not? But what about Vicky?'

'Don't worry about Vicky,' he said seriously. 'I finally managed to pin her down yesterday and we had a long talk about the difference between infatuation and love and the fact that one can become such a habit that you think it's the real thing.'

'And?' she prompted when he stopped there. 'I'm not good at solving cryptic clues.'

'And we both admitted that we'd been having serious doubts about what we were doing, and feeling so dreadfully guilty that we didn't want to see each other. Anyway, she seems to have someone else in her sights these days and I was having far too much fun going on horseback rides and sleeping on lumpy couches.'

'It is *not* lumpy,' she argued just for the sake of it, her heart seeming to float as the guilty weight was lifted.

'When did you last try sleeping on it?' he countered. 'Or perhaps it only seemed so uncomfortable because I couldn't ignore the fact that your very comfortable bed was just up those stairs.'

The memories of what they'd done in that bed was there in his darkening blue eyes but she couldn't let her thoughts drift in that direction. Not yet.

'So, you're not getting married any more,' she said doggedly, needing to get everything clear in her head before she could banish the guilt still hovering over her.

'Well, that depends,' he said and her heart took a dive towards her neatly shod feet. *Had* he and Vicky called a halt to their relationship or not?

Suddenly, to her surprise, he'd pulled her chair round to face towards him and she watched him go down on one knee in the prosaic surrounds of her kitchen.

'Frankie, I love you,' he declared in a husky voice that bore not a trace of teasing. 'Would you do me the honour of becoming my wife?'

'You love me?' she squeaked in disbelief as she stared into the face of the man she'd grown to love so much. 'But you can't. I'm older than you are and I've got so many responsibilities...Laura and Katie...and you're so...so...'

She couldn't find the words. How could she tell him that he was too handsome, too sexy, too *everything* to tie himself to someone who knew she was already past her prime?

'What I am is in love with you,' he said firmly, and this time she caught sight of a wicked twinkle. 'I think I fell in love with you when I saw you cleaning your car. Then you turned round with that hose in your hand and I saw the proof that you weren't wearing a bra under that wet T-shirt, and I *knew* I was in love.'

'Nick...!' She felt the heat searing her cheeks.

'Frankie, trust me. I love you and I love Laura and Katie and I love the idea that you're already carrying our first child. Please, say you'll—'

'*First?*' she spluttered. 'How many are you thinking of?'

'As many as you want, love,' he promised with his heart in his eyes. 'Just tell me you love me and that you'll marry me, soon.'

'Oh, Nick, of course I love you,' she capitulated, finally realising that the impossible seemed to be coming true. 'I fell in love with you before I knew you belonged to someone else and I've spent every day since feeling so guilty.'

'So you'll marry me?' he persisted. 'Before rheumatism sets in my knee?'

'Idiot! Oh, Nick, are you sure?'

'That's *lovable* idiot, if you remember, and as soon as you say yes I'll take a great deal of delight in showing you exactly how sure I am,' he promised, and drew her closer so that he could press a gentle kiss to her lips. 'Say yes,' he whispered, and feathered another tantalising kiss to follow the first. 'Say it, Frankie.'

'Yes,' she moaned, and he took full advantage of her parted lips, pulling her down into his arms to initiate caresses that could have only one result.

Frankie's last coherent thought before ecstasy overtook them was that she felt almost guilty for feeling so happy.

Modern Romance™
...seduction and
passion guaranteed

Tender Romance™
...love affairs that
last a lifetime

Sensual Romance™
...sassy, sexy and
seductive

Blaze™
...sultry days and
steamy nights

Medical Romance™
...medical drama on
the pulse

Historical Romance™
...rich, vivid and
passionate

29 new titles every month.

*With all kinds of Romance for
every kind of mood...*

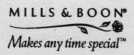

MILLS & BOON®

Makes any time special™

MAT4

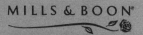

Medical Romance™

INNOCENT SECRET by Josie Metcalfe

Part 3 of Denison Memorial Hospital

Dr Joe Faraday is a man who keeps his heart hidden, and Nursing Sister Vicky Lawrence has her own secrets. She knows Joe wants her but something is holding him back. Vicky wonders if anything will tip him into her arms—and then her safety is put under threat…

HER DR WRIGHT by Meredith Webber

Dr Detective – Down Under

Rowena knew she was in love with her boss, Dr David Wright, and was beginning to suspect he felt the same. David was under suspicion for his wife's disappearance three years ago and Rowena desperately wanted to comfort him. But David refused to let her get involved—how could he offer her a future with his past hanging over him?

THE SURGEON'S LOVE-CHILD by Lilian Darcy

American surgeon Candace Fletcher feels the sizzling attraction as soon as Dr Steve Colton meets her off the plane in Australia—and the ensuing affair is passionate and intense. Then, just a few weeks before Candace is due to return home, the bombshell drops: she's pregnant!

On sale 1st March 2002

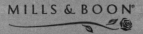

Treat yourself this Mother's Day to the ultimate indulgence

3 brand new romance novels and a box of chocolates

= only £7.99

Available from 15th February

MIRANDA LEE

Secrets & Sins

revealed

SEDUCED BY HER BODYGUARD AND STALKED BY A STRANGER...

Available from 15th March 2002

Available at most branches of WH Smith,
Tesco, Martins, Borders, Eason, Sainsbury's
and most good paperback bookshops.

0402/35/MB34

Starting Over

Another chance at love...
Found where least expected

PENNY JORDAN

Published 15th February

Available at most branches of WH Smith,
Tesco, Martins, Borders, Eason, Sainsbury's
and most good paperback bookshops.

FREE!

2 Books

and a surprise gift!

We would like to take this opportunity to thank you for reading this Mills & Boon® book by offering you the chance to take TWO more specially selected titles from the Medical Romance™ series absolutely FREE! We're also making this offer to introduce you to the benefits of the Reader Service™—

- ★ FREE home delivery
- ★ FREE gifts and competitions
- ★ FREE monthly Newsletter
- ★ Books available before they're in the shops
- ★ Exclusive Reader Service discount

Accepting these FREE books and gift places you under no obligation to buy; you may cancel at any time, even after receiving your free shipment. Simply complete your details below and return the entire page to the address below. *You don't even need a stamp!*

YES! Please send me 2 free Medical Romance books and a surprise gift. I understand that unless you hear from me, I will receive 4 superb new titles every month for just £2.49 each, postage and packing free. I am under no obligation to purchase any books and may cancel my subscription at any time. The free books and gift will be mine to keep in any case.

M2ZEB

Ms/Mrs/Miss/Mr ....Initials ....
BLOCK CAPITALS PLEASE

Surname ....

Address ....

....

....Postcode ....

Send this whole page to:
UK: The Reader Service, FREEPOST CN81, Croydon, CR9 3WZ
EIRE: The Reader Service, PO Box 4546, Kilcock, County Kildare (stamp required)